Praise for Mark Timlin

'A pure pulp vision closer to Spillane than Chandler. His books are bloody romances of the South London badlands'

John Williams

'As British as a used condom in a fogbound London taxi...'

Observer

'It is possible that South London contains some law abiding citizens in conventional relationships but they make no appearance in Timlin's immoral, wildly enjoyable books' *Times*

'The king of the British hard-boiled thriller' *Times*

'Full of cars, girls, guns, strung out along the high sierras of Brixton and Battersea, the Elephant and the North Peckham Estate, all those jewels in the crown they call Sarf London'

Arena

'Brit-pulp's tough guy prize goes to work on Mark Timlin's Nick Sharman' *Evening Standard*

'The most impressive aspect of Timlin's compressed style is the constant juxaposition of the witty and the tense ... Brilliantly conveys the dereliction and moral emptiness of the London underworld' *Sunday Times*

'Grips like a pair of regulation handcuffs' *Guardian*

'The mean streets of South London need their heroes tough. private eye Nick Sharman fits the bill' *Telegraph*

'Definitely one of the best' *Time Out*

'Timlin's South London is well drawn, full of dodgy boozers and villains, dodgier clubs and coppers, cemeteries and second-hand car dealers' *The Face*

Other books by Mark Timlin
A Good Year for the Roses 1988
Romeo's Tune 1990
Gun Street Girl 1990
Take the A-Train 1991
The Turnaround 1992
Hearts of Stone 1992
Zip Gun Boogie 1992
Falls the Shadow 1993
Ashes by Now 1993
Pretend We're Dead 1994
Paint It Black 1995
Find My Way Home 1996
Sharman and Other Filth (short stories) 1996
A Street That Rhymed at 3 AM 1997
Dead Flowers 1998
Quick Before They Catch Us 1999
All the Empty Places 2000

OTHERS
I Spied a Pale Horse 1999
Answers from the Grave 2004
Guns of Brixton 2010
as TONY WILLIAMS
Valin's Raiders 1994
Blue on Blue 1999
as JIM BALLANTYNE
The Torturer 1995
as MARTIN MILK
That Saturday 1996
as LEE MARTIN
Gangsters Wives 2007
The Lipstick Killers 2009

STAY
ANOTHER DAY

MARK TIMLIN

NO EXIT PRESS

First published in 2010 by No Exit Press,
P.O.Box 394, Harpenden, Herts, AL5 1XJ
www.noexit.co.uk

© Mark Timlin 2010

A CIP catalogue record for this book is available from the British Library.

This is a work of fiction. Names, characters, places, and incidents are either the
product of the author's imagination or are used fictitiously, and any resemblance
to actual persons, living or dead, businesses, companies, events or locales is
entirely coincidental.

ISBN 978-1-84243-328-7 (hardcover)

2 4 6 8 10 9 7 5 3 1

Typeset by Avocet Typeset, Chilton, Aylesbury, Bucks
Printed and bound in Great Britain by CPI Anthony Rowe, Chippenham, Wiltshire

For Lucy

PROLOGUE

It all started on a boiling summer bank holiday weekend at the start of the new Millennium when Nick Sharman – an ex-Metropolitan Police officer turned shady private detective – along with several others, robbed a bank in the City of London. Actually he wasn't one of the original robbers, but one of them had murdered the woman he loved, and he needed revenge – or closure as they call it nowadays – so he decided to rob the robbers. In the aftermath of the robbery the bank was blown up and totally destroyed, ruining much of the evidence. Collateral damage. He survived, the others didn't, and in the confusion he got away with several million pounds worth of currency and jewellery – more by luck than judgement.

Because of his relationship with the murdered woman and his knowledge of the major players in the robbery, he naturally came under suspicion as a prime suspect, and had some very bad moments as several coppers tried to identify him, all without any luck. But eventually it all got too hot for him in London, so the next year, he liquidated the jewels into cash, laid a bundle on his daughter Judith and did a runner to a small island in the Caribbean with a government who didn't object to dodgy immigrants as long as they were flush. He blended in fine with the collection of ex-military on the run from court martials, thieves, pirates and God knows who else, all of whom made a living fleecing tourists and smuggling various illegal goods on and off the island. Luckily he had enough cash that he didn't need to do anything crooked. Boring really.

But of course all things must pass.

PART ONE

1

It was three in the afternoon when I got the message. A typical afternoon for me, sitting under a sunshade by the pool I'd dug at the back of the little house I lived in, or trying to finish the *Telegraph* crossword in a two-day-old newspaper, which was how long they took to reach me. I didn't care. Old news suited me fine. Put everything in perspective, if you get my drift. The pool was fed by the ocean, and as I dipped my feet in the water little creatures would come and nibble at my toes. Very friendly, and if I put a net in later, I could haul a few out, toss them in boiling water and eat them for my evening meal with some rice and peas. Maybe not so friendly, but as I've discovered over the years, it's a harsh world. My only other companions on that afternoon, as most afternoons, were several feral cats that I fed, because I've always had an empathy for cats. They don't belong to anyone. Plus there was an old teddy bear. He was a reminder of past times, and someone I once loved who's buried three thousand miles away, in a cold grave in a cold country. But here, the air was warm, smelling of salt, fish and vaguely of spliff, which was one of the local cash crops.

So there I sat that afternoon, on one of the dozens of beautiful islands in the West Indies, thinking that this life would go on forever. But another fact I've discovered over the years is that things don't always go to plan.

I was still puzzling over three down when I heard the sound of an engine ripping through the afternoon quiet. I mostly ignored it. The coast road ran over a rise just a few hundred yards from my front door, so I often heard the sound of motors. But this one stopped, and I looked up to see Clive, the owner of a little bar and restaurant half a mile down the beach, come over the hill and jog in my direction. He was dressed similarly to me in a vest, shorts, flip-flops and shades, and his dreads flipped from side to side as he approached.

'Hey Clive,' I said. 'What's up?'

I expected him to tell me he had slaughtered a goat for curry and invite me round for supper, but instead he said, 'You got a phone call Jim. From England. She gonna call back in an hour.' He sounded excited at the thought.

He called me Jim because that's the name on my passport. James, that is. James Stark. But that's not my real name. And why don't I have my own phone? Because I don't care to talk to anyone much. More or less everything on the island is within walking distance. Everything I need that is. And as for mobiles, forget it. This was the original dead zone. There had been talk of a mast, but why? Anyway, I don't want a phone. Also, I have a past. But more of that later. And why the excitement? Well, I've been here for seven years, and this was my first phone call. That's what the excitement was about.

'She?' I said, trying to gather my thoughts. But I knew who *she* must be. My daughter Judith. One of only two people I'd given the phone number of Clive's restaurant to back in England.

'Yeah man. Sounded nice, but a little distraught. I've come to give you a ride.'

Distraught. I liked that. For all his dreadlocks and spliff and reggae, Clive was an educated man. Like me, he'd just wanted a quiet life.

I got up from the side of the pool, found *my* flip-flops and said. 'OK mate. Let's go.' I tried to sound cheerful but I felt a cold lump in my stomach that even the heat of the afternoon sun couldn't dispel.

Clive's little Honda bike was parked by the side of the road. Those single seaters were the vehicle of choice around the island. Clive jumped on and fired up the motor, and I perched on the luggage rack at the back, holding him tightly round his waist. It was a bloody uncomfortable way to travel, but even more uncomfortable to come off. Street pizza is a very unattractive injury, and the nearest doctor and hospital was a way off. The thirty-year-old ambulance was more often off the road than on. As I sat down I shifted the little pistol in the back pocket of my shorts. The pistol I'd grabbed when I heard the Honda's engine stop by my house. It doesn't do to take chances. Even here. Even after seven years. Like I said, I've got a past.

2

It was just a short trip thank God, made even shorter by Clive's driving style, which was flamboyant to say the least. Another reason I usually chose to walk when I popped into the bar for a drink and a bite to eat. He preferred the hooter to the brakes, and revved the little engine so hard it sounded like a banshee on its last journey to hell. So just a few minutes after we left my place he powered the bike onto the shell-covered parking space outside the beach shack he called home in a cloud of dust, scattering the chickens that supplied fresh eggs to the restaurant, skidded to a halt, and switched off.

The bar overlooked the ocean just like my house. The ocean could be a useful friend, but could be an enemy too, as several fisherman from the island had discovered to their peril. The building, if you could call it that, was made of scaffolding poles sunk deep into the sand, holding up a thatched roof, walled with wooden slats. The bar itself was fronted with mismatched stools, a tiny kitchen, and half a dozen tables and chairs that looked like they'd been rescued from a skip. But somehow, Clive and his business partner/chef Cyril had managed to create an ambience that brought people from all over the island, and further afield to talk and eat and drink in an atmosphere of friendliness that I'd rarely found anywhere else in the world. Of course it helped that Cyril had trained in a Michelin-starred restaurant back in England where he'd been born, and could cook like a dream. At the back was a more substantial building where Clive and Cyril were house mates, and entertained a variety of the female visitors who fell under their romantic spells.

That afternoon a few locals sat at the bar drinking from cans of Red Stripe and two tourists were drinking mai-tais at one of the tables and digging into plates of jerk chicken and sweet potatoes. It was just like a lot of afternoons I'd visited the place, but I knew it was different. It felt like the end of an era. A full stop in life's pageant.

I nodded a greeting as I went inside, and the locals raised their hands in salutes, as Clive went behind the bar and poured me my usual gin and tonic. He looked at the diver's watch on his wrist and said. 'Won't be long man.'

I said nothing back, just fished a cigarette from the battered pack in the side pocket of my shorts, lit it with my Zippo and took a long drink. This was one call I wasn't looking forward to taking.

Ten minutes later the phone rang with that peculiar sound that the phones made on the island, and my stomach lurched. Clive answered on the second ring, then held out the receiver to me. 'Here she is, Jim,' he said.

I walked into the short corridor that led to the kitchen under the gaze of the customers and took the phone from his hand. 'Hello,' I said in a voice that sounded strange to my own ears. 'Jim Stark.'

Then the voice of the only woman alive I loved came across half the world. 'Hello Dad.'

'Hello love, what do you need?'

'You,' she said in reply. 'I'm in trouble.'

'What kind of trouble?'

'Not on the phone.'

'Fair enough.'

'Can you come Dad?'

'Of course. You know I will.'

'You sure?'

'Try and stop me.'

'It's been so long.' And I heard her start to cry.

'Don't,' I said. I've never been good with outbursts of emotion. 'Please.' Aware of all the ears in the room listening to me.

'Sorry. It's not like me. I just need you Dad. When will you get here?'

'Just as soon as I can. Got a number for me?'

I gestured for Clive to pass me a piece of paper and a pen and I took down a London number. 'Give me a couple of days,' I said. 'It's complicated.'

'Quick as you can.'

'Trust me, love' I said. 'What time is it there?' I could never work it out.

'Morning. And cold. Very cold.'

'Smashing. Don't worry, I'll be there. Love you.'

'You too,' and she rang off. The phone was slippery with sweat when I put it back on the hook. And it wasn't just from the afternoon heat.

I went back to the bar and finished the G&T in one gulp. 'Once again please Clive,' I said.

'You leaving us man?' he asked as he dropped ice and a slice of lemon into a fresh glass, free poured the gin and topped it up with tonic.

'Looks like it.'

'Ladyfriend in trouble back in Blighty?'

'Daughter.'

'Jesus, man, you never said.'

'You never asked,' I said.

'Your business,' he said, shrugging.

'That's why I like this place. What happens elsewhere stays elsewhere.'

'Best for all concerned. When you off?'

'As soon as I can get sorted.'

'For good?'

'No idea,' I said, and I meant it.

'There'll always be a seat for you at the bar, you know that.'

'Cheers mate,' I said and raised my glass to him. For good? I thought. Doesn't sound like anything good to me.

3

By the time I left the bar the sun was sinking into the sea like a big red blister. I walked back home. I was just a bit unsteady on my feet, as I'd had several more G&T's, and a toke or two from a huge spliff from Cyril in the kitchen as he grilled me a red snapper with fat sweet potato chips and homemade lemon mayonnaise. He grilled *me* about the mystery phone call too and was as surprised as Clive that I had a daughter I'd never mentioned. But then, I'd never mentioned much about my life before the island. And anyway, as Judith hadn't told me exactly what kind of trouble she was in, I was no wiser than him.

By then the midges were swarming about. The locals call them no-see-ums because you don't until they start to bite. Some settled on my bare shoulder for an early supper. I should've been wearing a long sleeved shirt, but

I hadn't expected to be out so long. One of the few downsides of living in paradise are those damn bugs.

I just brushed them off as I walked, and I let my mind drift back to the past. Back to the dim and distant old life when I was in London.

Like I said before, my name's not James Stark. It's Nick Sharman, and I used to be a policeman until I resigned – before I was fired and prosecuted. I'd stolen a load of cocaine from the evidence locker at Brixton police station, and flogged what I didn't use. I had a wife and child to support and several expensive habits. Women, booze, fast cars and drugs mainly. I'm not proud of what I did, but it was the eighties, and things were different then. Also, I had a relationship with a very heavy south London villain named John Jenner. I did him some favours and he did me some back. Mostly, in small denomination used notes. Then I became a private detective. Don't laugh. See, I had no pension, a dodgy foot after being shot, and I still had some bad habits. A lot of people died during those years. My first and second wife, my unborn child, friends and enemies alike, some of them at my hand. Then finally, I got involved in a big robbery, where I was the last man standing. But I'm rich now, though you wouldn't know it from my lifestyle. I got out of London, and thought I'd stay out for the rest of my life. But now it looked like I had to go back. But to what?

And my daughter? Believe it or not, she's a copper too. I bet that raised some eyebrows at Hendon. But then she's not me. She's smart. Went to university, got a good degree and signed up to the Met. Fast track. She's still only in her twenties and she's a detective-inspector. That's what really worried me about the phone call. She shouldn't need me. And if you wonder how I know about her career without a single call in seven years, it's because the Caribbean bank where I've got my ill-gottens stashed away occasionally receives a postcard, which they hold for me. So they should. There's a lot of credit on my account. When I take a trip off the island I pop in and pick up my post. I don't answer them. It's just comforting to know what's going on, and that she still thinks enough about me to let me know how she's doing.

When I finally got back to my tiny house I fed the cats, grabbed a shirt and a beer, put Hank Williams on the CD player, lit a smoke bomb to keep the midges away, and went back to the pool. I fell asleep in a comfy old armchair next to the water as Hank and the sea lulled me off.

Tomorrow was another day, and something told me that my life here would never be the same again, no matter how much I wanted it to be.

4

At dawn, the sun rose over the horizon, zapping me in the face. I came to, still sitting in the chair. I got up to make a cup of tea which I drank as I walked across the beach towards the incoming tide, wondering whether it would be for the last time. When I'd finished I went back inside and squinted at myself in the mirror in the small bathroom. What I saw wasn't fit for travel. You see, I'd grown a beard and my hair was so long I usually tied it up in a ponytail. A real Robinson bleedin' Crusoe. Something would have to be done before I returned to civilisation and that meant Rita. I'd met her and her mother Gloria at Clive's early on in my stay on the island. Rita was the widow of one of the fishermen lost at sea a few years earlier. His body was never found, and there was an empty grave in the churchyard, with a wooden plaque above it.

She had two kids, a son and a daughter and ran a little hairdressers in town. We'd had a bit of a thing for a while; it fizzled out as those things do, but we'd stayed friends. We often met for a drink and a meal at the bar, and I knew she'd give me a trim if I popped round to her house, which was just a few minutes walk from Clive's place. I wasn't going to shave my beard completely – I was tanned nearly as dark as the natives of the island, and I would certainly cause some comment with half a dark and half a white face. And comment was the last thing I needed where I was going.

Next, I checked the safe I'd sunk into concrete under my bed. Inside was a bundle of cash in dollars and sterling, my other guns and ammunition. I had a nice little collection. The .22 auto I carried at all times, a .45 Glock and a 9mm Sig. There was a sports shop in the town where I'd bought them over the years. I didn't bother with licences and nor did the owner of the shop. Every so often I'd rent a jeep, buy a few watermelons, then drive up into the mountain in the centre of the island where it was quiet and shoot the shit out of the fruit. Very satisfying. I took out the money, folded it into a wallet, stuck the .22 next to the other weapons, and locked the safe again. There was no way I was going to try and take a weapon with me. I knew all about the increased security since 9/11. Christ, I remember that day so well. Time after time we'd watched the planes crash into the towers on the cranky old television in the bar, until we couldn't take any more, and by consensus had shut it down. There's only so much shit you can take before you become hardened to it.

Then I walked to Clive's. He was pottering around, and I asked if I could use the phone to call Jack. He was the owner, mechanic and pilot of the plane that hopped around the islands. We fixed a price that would keep him on the airstrip until I arrived later that day.

'You really leaving?' asked Clive as he cooked me ham and eggs, which he served with black coffee laced with a slug of dark rum.

'Yes,' I said.

'Coming back?'

'I still don't know.'

'Remember what I said about the seat.'

'I will mate.'

'We'll miss you Jim.'

I couldn't leave it like that. 'Listen Clive,' I said. 'You and Cyril, and everyone here have been such good friends to me, I can't leave you with a lie. My name's not Jim.'

'I think we figured that one out years ago. But like I said before, your business.'

'Yeah. I imagine it was that obvious. Anyway, my name's Nick,' and I stuck out my hand.

He took it in his. 'Pleased to meet you Nick,' he said. 'Clive.'

'Clive,' I replied, and hugged him tight. 'Now listen,' I said. 'You've got a spare key to the house. Feed the cats and look out for the place will you?'

He nodded.

'It's bought and paid for. And if I don't come back soon, it's yours.'

'I'll guard it with my life,' he said.

'No need to go quite that far. There's a safe under the bed.' I wrote down the combination on a scrap of paper. 'There's all sorts inside. Probably illegal some of them. Do with them as you see fit.'

He nodded.

'Here's some money for my tab and the cat food,' I said, pulling out some notes.

He waved it away. 'Tab can wait 'til you come back. We'll have a party. You can pay after that.'

'It'll be my pleasure. Where's Cyril?'

'At the market.'

'I'll catch him before I go. I'm off to Rita's. Get spruced up for the journey.'

'You could use it man,' he said, laughing.

'Cheers. And one other thing.' I put my old teddy on the bar, that I'd carried up in my pocket. 'Put this fella somewhere. Somewhere to keep an eye on you lot.'

He grinned. '*My* pleasure,' he said, placing the bear onto a shelf next to the TV set.

5

When I'd finished my breakfast I headed for Rita's. She was getting the kids, Jacey and Little Gloria, ready for school. It was the last few days of term before the Christmas break, and they were going crazy, all excited about the play they were going to be in that day. When I knocked on her back door she shooed them off to clean their teeth. 'What can I do for you big man?' she asked. She never called me Jim. I'd told her my real name when we were an item, but she knew not to call me that either.

'I'm going back to England,' I said.

'So I heard.' I couldn't read her expression.

'I couldn't leave without seeing you, and I can't go looking like this. I wondered if you had your scissors handy.'

'Never without them. Sit down, I'll get a towel.'

I sat on the hard kitchen chair as she brought me coffee, and then started. My hair's still thick, thank God, but flecked with a lot of grey. 'How you want it?' she asked, running her hands through it.

'Keep it long, but stylish, you know.'

'Trust me.'

As there was no mirror in front of me I had no choice but to do just that and soon the floor was covered in hair. She stood back, cocked her head, and said. 'That'll do. Now for the beard.'

'Make it short please.'

It only took a few minutes and she scrutinised me again. 'Yeah,' she said. 'You're almost handsome.'

I shucked off the towel and went to the bathroom to look in the mirror. Pretty good. I hardly recognised myself. There was no beard on James Stark's passport photo, but it was old and I figured it would pass muster. If not I was for the cells as soon as I got into Heathrow – but that was a chance I had to take.

The kids had been racing in and out as she worked, but eventually they calmed down enough to speak. 'I'm the queen,' said Little Gloria proudly to me. 'In our play. Will you come?'

'I can't sweetheart,' I replied. 'I'm going on a trip.'

'Very far?'

'Yes.'

'Can't you stay another day?'

'Sorry,' I said. 'I'd love to. But I have a daughter too. Just like you. She needs me.'

Rita showed no surprise. I'd told her about Judith too.

'Then you have to go,' Little Gloria said.

I nodded.

'Will you come back?'

'If I can.'

'No more questions,' scolded Rita. 'Get off now, and I'll see you at lunch for the play. Your costume's OK?'

'Lovely,' said Little Gloria and kissed her mother, then me. She examined me critically, and said, 'you look different to me.'

'I hope that goes for a lot of people,' I replied as the children ran out of the house.

Jacey stopped at the door. 'Merry Christmas,' he said.

'The same to you,' I said back, shaking his small hand.

'So listen big man,' said Rita. 'You take care. I hate good-byes. Just get the hell out of here.'

'Is that a tear I see in your eye?' I asked.

She shook her head, but she lied, and I must confess I filled up too. I regretted the fact that we hadn't made more of an effort, but that was history. 'Listen,' I said. 'I was going off island next week to get you a Christmas present. And the kids, and Gloria too. Sorry, but I can't now.'

'No problem.'

'Yes it is.' I took out my wallet, and peeled off a lump of cash. 'Get them all something from me will you? I know it's not the same, but I had no idea this would happen.'

She tried to shrug off the money, but I said, '*Rita*. Take

it please. Not just for them but for me. You're all important to me. More important than I realised until now.'

'OK, big man,' she said. 'As it's you.' The tears were rolling down her face freely now.

'I love you,' I whispered, embracing her in a big bear hug and kissing her on both cheeks. She shooed me away, and as I walked down the path I wondered if I'd ever see her again.

6

I walked back to the house, had a quick shower to get the loose hair off and decided what to take for my journey. I had a leather holdall that I filled with toiletries, what there were of them, socks I hadn't worn for years, and underwear. I knew all about these new rules about carry-on luggage from tourists at the bar complaining about them, so I took nothing else. No scissors, no nail files. Then I had to choose what to wear. It wasn't much of a choice. Jeans, cowboy boots, a Hawaiian shirt and a tan linen jacket. Cigarettes, lighter, passport and wallet and I was ready to go.

I said ta-ta to the cats, hoisted the holdall on my shoulder, locked up and left. Seven years, and it took only a few minutes to quit the place.

I headed for Clive's for the last time, the boots killing

my feet after going almost barefoot for so long. When I walked into the bar there were jeers of derision at my appearance but I took them like a man. I went into the kitchen to bid goodbye to Cyril. He was cooking something gorgeous featuring crab and lemongrass, and I wished I could stay for lunch. Back in the bar, Clive said, 'You're limping man. How you going to get to the strip?'

'Painfully,' I replied.

'Hey Horace,' he called to one of the regulars. 'You got your truck?'

'Sure.'

'Then give this man a ride to Jack's.'

'I just got here man,' he moaned,

'And you're just leaving again. Have a heart.'

I pulled out the last of my local currency and slapped it on the bar. 'A drink for the house,' I said. 'And a bottle of rum for Horace.'

There were cheers, more jeers, and farewells. But I think it was the drink for the house that did it, rather than my leaving.

'See ya fellas,' I said to the assorted punters, as I left with Horace to find his ancient pick-up. 'Merry Christmas and a happy new year.'

It was only ten minutes drive to the airstrip where Jack was waiting with his little twin-engined Cessna.

He was ex-RAF, had flown in the first Gulf war, resigned and headed for the island to find some peace. He hadn't like bombing civilians, and who could blame him.

I paid him in dollars, which he appreciated, and

climbed into the cramped cabin. Jack checked his instruments, fired up the engines and we were off. I looked back at the paradise that had been my home for the last seven years as we headed away over the water, bound for Jamaica and a big silver bird that would take me back to civilisation – if you could call it that.

I speculated exactly what I would find there. Nothing pleasant, I was sure of that.

7

Flying with Jack was not dissimilar to riding with Clive. Both seemed to have a disregard for human life, including their own. Jack flew so low over the sea that I could almost smell the ocean, and I swear the waves lapped at the cabin. But if anyone ever protested, he'd just go even lower, and he always delighted in telling the story of pulling fish out of the undercarriage when he got to his destination. How true that was I don't know, but I just stayed silent and let him get on with it.

We touched down less than an hour later. I shook his hand, and watched as he turned the plane and headed back to the island. I wished I was returning with him, but instead picked up my bag and headed for the terminal to get a ticket to London.

I got lucky. There was a direct flight to Heathrow that

evening. 9.52 to arrive the next day at 12.45, so I booked a one way ticket. First class. If I was going to be led off in handcuffs, at least I wanted to get there in comfort. I used James Stark's Black American Express card to pay for the flight and headed to the first class lounge to wait. I had to put my bag into the hold, which suited me fine. I settled down with a pile of magazines, the new Harlan Coben and that day's *Telegraph*, bummed a pen off the woman who served me complimentary champagne and got stuck into the crossword. Some things never change.

It was a long flight, but I didn't care, safely tucked up as I was in a large leather reclining seat with plenty of legroom, in an almost empty first class cabin, I enjoyed free booze and a very decent dinner, plus the attentions of two tasty looking flight attendants, one male, one female. I think they assumed I was a superannuated middle-aged rock star heading home for the holidays to a number of ex-wives and several trustafarian children – just the impression I was trying to give.

As we headed over the English coast, the pilot gave us our landing time and the weather in London. Cold, as per usual. I wished I'd worn something more suitable. Still, I could sort that out when I got there.

We circled over the city for a few minutes and I looked down at East London where the river ran through it like a silver snake. Canary Wharf caught a ray of sunshine, and I was amazed at the changes. So many more towers than when I left. And I spotted The Gherkin, which I'd only seen in photographs. I knew I was heading back to a town

I'd barely recognise, and the sinking feeling in my stomach wasn't just from the plane's descent.

I was one of the first off the aircraft, collected my single bag and headed for the exits through the green channel. No one stopped me. No one gave me as much as a second glance. Home and dry. The draught through the doors of the terminal was as cold as Christmas. Maybe because it was.

But the people. Christ, during the last six years, the biggest crowd I'd seen was at Gloria's seventieth birthday party. Maybe a hundred people gathered together. But this place was rammed and I started to freak out, getting outside as quickly as possible to light up a cigarette and calm me down.

The airline had offered me a complimentary limo ride to London, but I wanted to cut the thread that attached me to the island as quickly as possible, so I crushed the cigarette after just a puff or two, and headed for the taxi rank.

8

Of course there was a queue at the rank, and I stood there shivering as a fine drizzle began to fall. Welcome to London!

Eventually it was my turn and I fell into the back seat of a taxi which thankfully had a working heater. 'West End,' I said. There was a big THANK YOU FOR NOT SMOKING sign in front of me, so I didn't. It was too early to upset the natives. Plenty of time for that later.

'Whereabouts?' asked the cabbie, a bullet headed bloke of about forty.

'Somewhere I can get a coat and some other stuff,' I said. 'I'm bleedin' freezin''

'You don't look like you're dressed for the weather,' he said, as he put the cab into gear and drove off. 'Come far?'

'Dubai,' I lied.

'Warm there?'

'Warm enough.'

'Home for Christmas?'

'That's about it. Rush job for the firm.'

'Oil?'

'Minerals.'

'Nice work if you can get it.'

'Yeah.'

'You travel a lot then?'

'All over the place,' I answered.

'Must be lonely.'

'I manage.'

Typical London cabbie, didn't know when to stay quiet. 'Been away long?'

'Long enough, as they say.'

'It's all change round here. Even got a new mayor.'

'Yeah, I know.'

'Got rid of that bleedin' Livingstone.'

'Red Ken.'

'That's the bugger.'

'I know one thing that's changed for sure,' I said.

'What's that then?'

I squinted through the glass between me and him. 'The price of taxi fares,' I said.

Oh, how we both laughed.

'Still got family here?' he said when he calmed down.

'Just a daughter.'

'How old?'

'Twenties,' I said.

'You're lucky. Mine's fourteen. Right little madam. She's just had her tongue pierced.'

'Dear, dear.' I remembered Judith at that age. She did a runner from home and ended up with a bunch of travellers on the music festival circuit.

The motorway into town hadn't changed much, except for a bus and taxi lane I didn't remember, but was thankful for, as the traffic was crazy and backed right up to the services. Of course the cabbie sailed through, and across the flyover, before we hit more traffic coming up to Hammersmith.

'Bleedin' mug punters,' he said, as we sat in the queue.

'Busy,' I replied

'What do you expect? Only two more Saturdays 'til Christmas. Now, what about this coat?'

'Could try Oxford Street?' I said.

'Don't bother. I was there earlier. Couldn't move. There's a decent place on the Strand. Next to the Savoy.'

'Fine,' I said. 'Anything warm would do me. And I need a hotel.'

'Got nothing booked? Christ mate, you'll be lucky.'

'Surprise visit,' I said. 'Not planned. On the hurry up. I need somewhere decent.'

'You'll have to ring round.'

'No phone.'

'No mobile?' I saw him give me a funny look in the mirror.

'Left it behind, would you believe. Sitting on the

dresser. Told you, I was in a hurry. I'll pick up another tomorrow.'

'I don't know what to say mate.'

'You must know places,' I said, feeling foolish.

'Cost ya.'

'That's OK, I'm on exes. Firm'll cough up.'

'Didn't your office book you something then?'

This bloke was sharper than I gave him credit for. I realised I was out of practice. I'd have to watch it. 'Short term contract,' I said. 'No time. Just get on a plane. I'd be obliged if you could wait for me when I'm in the shop. I'll make it worth your while.'

I saw him clock me again. The faded jeans, loud shirt and jacket, and just a battered leather bag as luggage. I didn't blame him for being a bit suss. He hesitated, then said. 'Listen. I'll do you a favour. I'll phone a few hotels where I know the people on reception.'

'That's terrific,' I said. 'But I want somewhere central. And I'll pay whatever. Maybe The Savoy itself.'

'Closed for redecoration mate,' he said. 'Didn't you know?'

Actually I had read something about it, but I'd forgotten. 'Course,' I said. 'Brain's not working today.'

'Never mind,' he said. 'I'll get you something.'

I got two fifties out of my wallet. The clock was already up in the thirty quid region, and it was ticking steadily. Taxi fares *had* rocketed in my absence. I passed the cash through the divider, and he looked at the notes suspiciously. 'Something wrong?' I asked.

'Lots of snides about,' he replied, studying the money against the windscreen.

'They're OK, mate,' I said. 'Got them from my bank this morning.' Another lie.

'Fair enough,' he said as he stuffed them in his pocket, saw a gap in the traffic and shot through.

Christ, I thought. Things have changed. Cabbies knocking back fifty pound notes – whatever next?

We swung through west London and eventually arrived at the old tailor's in the Strand. 'I'll park round the next corner,' he said, archly.

'I might be a while.'

'No problem,' he replied, grinning. 'Meter's on.'

I hoped he wouldn't just pocket the cash and piss off, so I took my bag, just in case. 'What's your name?' I asked as I got out.

'Stew,' he said.

'Jim,' I replied. 'See you later.'

'I'll be here. By the way, what's your surname? For the hotel.'

'Stark,' I said.

'No probs, I'll getcha somewhere.'

'Thanks.'

I went into the shop, which was pretty quiet, being a bit off the beaten track for Christmas shopping, and was immediately buttonholed by a lovely young thing in a three piece worsted, pink shirt and striped tie. 'Help you sir,' he said, giving my outfit a dirty look, one eyebrow raised.

'I need a couple of suits, some shirts, ties, sweaters, gloves, shoes, overcoat and a scarf,' I said.

Blimey, he almost bit my hand off.

'Overcoat?' he said, no doubt thinking of his commission.

'Cashmere,' I said back.

'No problem.'

And that was us.

It took half an hour for me to be outfitted in two beautiful whistles, one single, one double breasted. Half a dozen button down cotton oxford shirts in white, blue, pink and violet. Two cashmere jumpers in dark blue, a black cashmere scarf, leather gloves, and a fabulous navy cashmere nanny with a velvet collar, finished off with a pair of soft, black leather slip-ons with thick rubber soles to save my aching feet. The total price was something in the region of three grand. At least Simon, my helpful assistant, chucked in half a dozen silk ties gratis. He parcelled up my kit and I left. There was a fat hole in Stark's American Express but I was feeling as warm as toast.

Stew was waiting where he said, and he straight away informed me I had a room in the Park Lane Hotel, which was going to cost me plenty.

'Ask for Pierre at the desk,' he said. 'He's the major domo. And he'll need a bung.'

At least *some* things didn't change.

9

We shot round to Park Lane where Stew dropped me off in front of the hotel. The clock was up to ninety quid by then, so I let him keep the ton and added a twenty pound note for his troubles. 'Receipt?' he asked, as I collected my bags.

I was about to say no, when I remembered I was supposed to be on expenses, and answered in the affirmative.

He wrote me out a receipt and added a mobile number. 'In case you need to get around,' he said, and winked. 'I'm working over Christmas. Anything to get out of the bloody house.'

'Call anytime,' he went on. 'And if there's anything you need...' He didn't say more. Just my luck to get a dodge cabbie. But then he might come in useful.

I got out of the cab and a gent in livery dived for my

bags. 'Pierre,' I said. 'He's expecting me.'

The doorman nodded and led the way through revolving doors and up to the desk. I had nothing less than a fiver, so I handed one over and he saluted as a big bloke in black jacket and striped trousers hove into view. 'Pierre,' said the doorman and headed back outside.

'*Monsieur*,' said Pierre.

'Stark. James Stark,' I said. 'You got a call about me.'

'Ah, Stewart,' said Pierre. '*Oui*. Your room is ready. How long do you envision staying?'

'No idea,' I said. 'A few days.'

'Excellent. This room is yours tonight and tomorrow. If you wish to stay longer we will have to move you.' He told me the price for bed without breakfast per night. It would have kept me alive on the island for a month, but what the hell.

'No problem,' I said. 'I haven't got much with me. Just had to do some shopping in fact.'

Pierre didn't seem fazed by my lack of luggage, and called a bellboy to take what I had. He handed me a key card and asked for my credit card details in return. As all that was happening I slipped him a fifty pound note, which at least *he* had the good grace not to check.

The boy took me and my stuff to one of the lifts and up to my room, and very decent it was too. King size bed, flat screen TV, DVD/CD player and a view of the park from a tiny balcony. And thank Christ, it was warm. The boy got another fiver from my depleted stash, and at last I was alone.

The bed looked inviting, but I needed to get in touch with Judith, and for that I needed a mobile. I wasn't going to use the hotel phone. I was leaving a trail as wide as a motorway, and I didn't need to make it any bigger. So, in coat, scarf, gloves, and my new shoes I headed up Park Lane to Oxford Street.

Stew had been right. If I thought the terminal at Heathrow was packed, the stony hearted stepmother as the street was sometimes known, took the biscuit. The wide pavements were full, with coppers with loud hailers herding the stressed shoppers and tourists, and the road itself was jammed with more buses than I'd ever seen in my life.

Eventually, I found a phone shop and purchased a pay-as-you-go mobile that did everything but make the tea. Music, video, still photos, not that I thought I'd need half of it. The works. It came with a tenner of credit, and the little Asian geezer who sold it to me got it up and running in a few minutes. Another lump on the card, and it was mine.

I found a side street that was a little less crowded, stood inside someone's doorway and phoned the number Judith had given me. She answered quickly. 'Judith,' I said.

'Dad. Where are you?'

'Oxford Street.'

'London?'

'Of course.'

'That was quick. Thank you, I'm so glad you're here.'

'Where are *you*?'

'Camden. At home. Don't come here.'

'No worries. I don't even know where you live.'

'Course not. Sorry. Listen. Walk up towards Tottenham Court Road. Just past HMV there's a turning on the left. There's a funny pub down there. It's dark inside – full of Goths. No one will look for us there. I'll be half an hour.'

'Fine,' I said. But she'd gone.

10

I couldn't face battling the crowds all the way down Oxford Street, so I cut through the back doubles and found the boozer, with a load of people outside smoking in the cold. I bodyswerved past them and entered the warmth of the pub. I reckoned Judith had been right. No one would look for us in here. My cashmere overcoat seemed well out of place as the sartorial order of the day was leather and lace, denim and velvet. Mostly black of course, including the nail polish and lipstick, but with a sprinkling of red just for contrast. And that was just the geezers. And the music. I didn't recognise any of it. But it wasn't Hank Williams, that's for sure.

I ordered a pint of lager from the girl behind the bar, and was so used to dropping bungs that day that I almost gave her a fiver as a tip. I gave her a smile instead, which when she returned it showed a mouthful of enough metal to be recycled into a small car. I found an empty table at the back, but there was no ashtray, so I went back to the bar. 'Got an ashtray darling?' I asked.

'No smoking in here' she said, without a smile this time, and pointed at a notice on the door with an inch long fingernail. 'Where you been?'

'Sorry,' I said. 'I forgot.' Course there was a smoking ban everywhere in England. I'd read about it, laughed on my little island and sparked another cigarette at Clive's bar. I wasn't laughing now. That's why all those people were outside. Rebels or what? I wasn't about to join them, so I just went back to the table and just sat and waited for my daughter.

She arrived about ten minutes later wearing a camel hair coat with a black wool beret pulled over her hair. She saw me and came to the table. I stood and embraced her and she took off her hat to let her blonde hair loose. She looked fabulous. The hair had skipped a generation, but just looking at her face I knew she was my child, all grown up. 'Drink?' I asked.

'Jack Daniels and water,' she replied as she sat. My daughter all right.

I bought her drink and another pint for me and sat opposite her. 'It's wonderful to see you,' I said.

'Is it, Dad?' she asked, looking worried.

'Course it is love. I missed you.'

'You might not say that when I tell you what's up.'

'Whatever it is, you can tell your old Dad.'

'I'm on suspension. Full pay.'

'What's the charges?'

'Corruption, theft. Oh, and murder,' she laughed bitterly.

'Do what? Who got killed?'

'One of my covert human intelligence sources.'

'Do what?' It sounded like gibberish to me.

'An informant. What you'd have called a snout.'

'Oh, right. Was he any good?'

'The best. He got me my last promotion.'

'Nonsense then. You don't kill the golden goose.'

'Some people think I did.'

'And what theft?' I asked.

'He'd withdrawn money from his bank. Five grand. Gone.'

'You don't need money.'

'Course I don't. But my guv'nors don't know that. The money you left me was hardly legally obtained was it? I couldn't exactly declare it.'

'Good point,' I said. 'Then why haven't you been nicked?'

'Bad for the reputation of the service.'

'Service my arse. It was always a force. No wonder it's gone down the pan.'

'How do you know?'

'We get papers on the island.'

'You're not still reading the bloody *Telegraph*? Always bitching about us.'

'Good crossword though.'

She just sighed.

'So Judith, what can I do?'

'Help me.'

'You know I will. But why me?'

'Because you do things other people won't. And besides, I've always had to live with your reputation.'

'Like father like daughter eh?'

She nodded that time.

'I bet you had to put up with some shit.'

'You could say that.'

'Then I'm all yours.'

'Thanks. Aren't you going to ask me?'

'Ask you what?'

'If I did it.'

'Don't be daft love. I couldn't care less anyway. I'd help you if you came in here dripping with his blood.'

'Same old Dad.'

'Less of the old.'

Finally, I got a smile out of her.

We decided, or rather Judith did, that it wasn't wise to be together in town, but before she left she gave me her mobile phone number, plus her address. A flat in a street off Camden High Road. She told me it was part of a recent conversion in a terraced street. A garden flat, which was her pride and joy. I gave her my mobile number, and where I was staying. We arranged to meet on Monday morning in Oxford, well out of the Met area. She'd drive, I'd go by train. She said she'd give me all the grisly details then. I claimed exhaustion, and the need for sleep for the delay. But in fact I needed to think about what Judith had told me. My girl was a different person from the one I'd left behind all those years ago. She left first and I had another pint. Then I went back to the hotel and a warm bed. As I lay in a strange room, in what was turning out to be a strange city that I hardly recognised, I felt a terrible homesickness for my house on the island. Also, I decided I needed a weapon. I felt undressed without one. But that could wait until tomorrow. Eventually I fell into a troubled sleep, where a sense of nameless dread haunted my dreams.

11

The places I knew where guns were for sale were Brixton, Clapham and Hackney. Or at least that used to be the case. My face was too well known for south London, even with the beard. Even after all this time. Anyway, I was conceited enough to think so. So, I thought a trip up the Wick was on the cards. But not in cashmere. Which was why, after a good night's sleep and a breakfast in the hotel that was fit for a king – and cost me a king's ransom – I dived up Notting Hill on Sunday morning and bought a secondhand leather jacket so distressed it almost wept, some heavy steel-capped boots and a couple of sweatshirts, one hooded, that appeared to be the style *de jour*.

I stayed in my room all day after that, eating from room service, reading the Sunday papers and checking out the hundreds of channels on the TV.

I set off when it was dark, wearing boots, jeans, my new jacket, both sweatshirts, a scarf and gloves. I thought I looked the part, whatever the part was, and besides, it was still bloody cold.

Of course there was still no tube in Hackney. I considered calling Stew and his cab, but thought better of it. Instead I found a lobster on Park Lane and asked to get dropped off at Liverpool Street station. It's a bit of a hike, but I needed to get reacclimatised to London, and shanksies is still the best way.

Blimey, but I was in for a shock. What used to be deserted back streets around Spitalfields were buzzing. There were new bars and restaurants everywhere and the streets were packed with art students in outlandish clothing and tourists doing Jack the Ripper tours. This wasn't how I remembered it. Times had changed for sure and left me washed up on the beach.

I wandered up past Victoria Park, and into Hackney proper. I was looking for just the right kind of pub. Somewhere where the villains hung out.

The first couple were all wrong. Kids getting into the spirit of Christmas with Slade on the jukebox. Then, when I got deeper into the back streets, I found just the place. The Christmas decorations were dusty, and some of the fairy lights were blown, the music was old soul, and the drinkers looked like they were glued to their seats. Except for one corner, where there were three young black blokes, dripping with gold.

Stereotyping? Sure. Don't blame me. It's the way I was brought up.

I bought a pint of Stella and sort of drifted in their direction. They clocked me right away. Did I still look like a copper?

They were all young but they were big men, shaven heads, sweats and jeans or combat pants. I drew up a stool, and there we were. Four little hoodies, all in a row.

I knew they were talking about me, looking suspicious and throwing hard glances in my direction. But I'd come here to get what I needed, and I had to at least *try* to get it.

When the one closest gave me a glare, I nodded in a friendly way, but he just turned, said something I couldn't hear and they all laughed. Not a pleasant sound. There was no way I could take these three boys if anything kicked off. It would be the London hospital for me and how would that help Judith? The geezer I'd nodded at stood up to call for more drinks and bumped me hard with his elbow. 'Watch it man,' he said with a growl.

'Sorry mate,' I said. Mistake.

'You're not my mate.'

'No,' I said 'Sorry.'

'You gay man?'

'No,' I replied.

'You look gay, man. Batty bwoy.'

'No,' I said.

'He not gay,' he said loudly to his friends. Loud enough to turn heads from other drinkers.

Jesus, I thought. This could get nasty. 'Sir,' I said. 'I meant no offence. I just came in for a quiet drink. No trouble.'

'You got trouble man,' said the bloke.

'Look,' I said, holding my palms up in an attempt to placate him. 'I've been away. I'm back for Christmas. Just looking round places I used to know.'

'You know this place?'

'I used to, years ago.'

'So where you been. Jail?'

'Not with this tan,' I smiled, trying to disarm him.

'Where then?'

I told him the name of the island.

The bloke furthest from me fixed me with a look that made the other one appear like an old pal. 'You taking the piss?' he said.

Christ, what now, I thought. 'No,' I said.

'I come from there.'

The middle one said. 'No way man. You come from the *Arethusa* estate on Morning Lane.'

'My family man. You better not be lying.' That was to me.

'No,' I said. 'I was there Friday.'

'Who you know?'

'Clive and Cyril from my local bar. Gloria and her family. Loads of people.'

'Gloria?'

'Yeah. Gloria and Rita.'

'Auntie Rita, Granny Gloria. You pulling my plonker?'

'No. Me and Rita, we had a bit of a thing.'

'You and Rita. He ain't gay man. Rita's... ' He didn't know what to say.

'What's your name?' I asked.

'Arnold.'

'Christ. Gloria's got a photo of you on her sideboard. I was at her seventieth birthday.'

'Man,' he said. 'I don't believe this. How are Rita's kids?'

'Jacey and Little Gloria? Doing well. Learning their ABC's and being polite. They're in the nativity play this year.'

'Well fuck me,' said Arnold. 'Buy this man a drink. What can we do for you?'

'Well, as it goes,' I said. 'I need a gun.'

12

Now, that was a conversation stopper if ever I heard one. 'Do what?' said the biggest bloke.

'A gun,' I repeated.

'What you want a piece for?' asked Arnold.

'Personal protection. Someone in my family has problems.'

'What kind of problems?' The big bloke again.

'Bad ones. She's in big trouble.'

'She?' said Arnold.

'My daughter. She's a copper. I used to be.'

'Told ya,' said the other bloke who hadn't spoken so far.

'And why us?' asked the big bloke. 'We look like we've got guns?'

'I took a chance.'

'You sure did. We nearly caned you.'

'My lucky day.'

'You can say that again,' said Arnold. 'But if you're setting us up... .' He didn't finish.

'If I set you up, I set myself up.'

'And why should we help five-oh?'

'I'd help Gloria, or Rita, or two dozen other people on the island. They took me in and didn't ask questions.'

'Constable Yapp still there?' asked Arnold.

'Inspector Yapp,' I corrected him. 'He's coming up for retirement. I have a drink with him now and then.'

'Jesus. I went to visit once and he chased me for stealing pineapples.'

'Did he catch you?' I asked.

'The hell he did. I was fast in them days. But he got me later.'

'It's a small place. What did he do?'

'Boxed my ears.'

'Sounds about right.'

We all laughed, even the silent one.

'So what's your name man?' asked the big bloke.

'Jim,' I replied, and stuck out my hand.

He took it after a moment. 'Skin,' he said. 'Latimer.' He nodded at the silent one. 'What do you reckon boys?'

'How much dough you got?' said Arnold, and I figured I was in. Or else they were going to rob me, kill me, and dump me in the River Lea.

13

After that, we took more drinks over to a quiet table and got down to business. 'What kind of gun do you want?' asked Skin.

'Not some east Europe knockoff. A forty five's my favourite. A real frightener.'

'Glock?'

'Or Colt. 1911. I'm used to them.'

'Seven shots man,' he said with a sneer.

'I like 'em. Anyway, I don't intend to kill more than seven people at once.'

'You sure of yourself,' said Arnold. 'You ever killed anyone?'

I didn't answer.

'Reckon he has,' said Latimer. 'Why else he hiding out in that little place?'

'Who said I was in hiding?' I said.

He shrugged. He didn't say much, but I knew he'd sussed me out.

'OK, OK,' said Skin. 'Who cares. You want a 1911, we get you one. Not something I'd use, but it's your arse.'

'Plus ammo?'

'Not much good without. A box of fifty do you?'

'For now.'

'Man's ambitious,' said Arnold, and we all laughed like old mates.

'How much?' I asked. This was going to be the tricky part. Maybe they had access to weapons, and maybe not. Three against one. Bad odds, and I wasn't getting any younger.

'A monkey,' said Skin.

'That's a lot,' I replied. Maybe, maybe not. I was out of touch.

'It's not fucking Tesco,' he said. 'Take it or leave it. We've got places to be, ladies to see.'

'When?'

'Right now. You give us the cash, we go and get the goods.'

'And I sit here and wait?'

'The man don't trust us,' said Skin.

'Sure I do,' I said. 'But you know...'

'Let him be,' said Arnold. 'I'll stick around. He can tell me all about Granny Gloria and Auntie Rita.'

'And the bloke who bitch slapped you,' said Latimer with a big grin.

'Yeah. And him too,' said Arnold, 'But it was years ago man.'

So that was it. Job done.

'Cash,' said Skin.

'I'll be right back,' I said, getting up and heading for the gents. If they followed me and gave me a kicking, they'd be a grand richer. Which was exactly how much I had down my Calvins.

But they didn't. I found a noxious stall without a lock, pulled out my wallet, separated five hundred quid from my stash and went back to the table. I slipped the money into Skin's hand, and he and Latimer left.

I bought Arnold a drink and regaled him with tales of the island. What a pleasant evening it was turning out to be.

It would be the last for quite a while.

14

Skin and Latimer were back within half an hour. Skin was carrying a heavy looking Sainsbury's carrier bag. Well, he *had* said it wasn't Tesco. He handed it over and I peered inside. There was a box of .45 calibre full metal jackets and a battered looking Colt 1911A. 'I'll have to have a squint,' I said.

He shrugged, and once again I headed for the gents. I stood in the stall with my back against the door and hauled out the pistol. I worked the action that seemed smooth, peered down the barrel that was dusty but clear, dropped out the empty magazine and tested the spring, which was good and firm, fiddled with the safeties until I was satisfied. The blueing was worn off the barrel and the grips were discoloured, but it wasn't in a beauty contest, so I put it back in the bag and returned to the bar. 'Looks

OK,' I said. 'History?'

'Don't worry man,' said Skin. 'If you get nicked with that you'll go down, history or no history.'

He was right about that for sure, but I didn't intend to be nicked with or without the gun. 'Fair enough,' I said. 'Listen, I'm going to split. Things to do, ladies to see.'

'Pleasure,' said Skin. 'Anytime. They know us here. If you need anything, just come by.'

'I'll remember that,' I said, and with a tip to an imaginary hat, and a Merry Christmas all round, I left.

I walked away fast, then saw a cab by the station, hailed it and asked for Marble Arch. The ride was swift and I walked down to the hotel, went to my room, field stripped the gun, cleaned it as best I could and loaded the magazine. The gun was old but someone had cared for it pretty well. It was oiled and the action worked nicely. I stored it in my leather bag under the stiffener at the bottom, emptied the ammo box into the plastic bag, which went next to the gun, tore the box into tiny pieces and went for an evening stroll, discarding the bits in drains and skips as I went. I returned to the hotel for an expensive tot of Glenfiddich in the almost deserted bar and went to bed, well satisfied.

15

At six am, my phone went off, lighting up the ceiling like a UFO ready for take off. I scrambled for the instrument on top of the cupboard next to my bed and said, 'Yes?'

'Dad it's me,' said Judith.

Just as well I thought, as she was the only person with the number. 'I've been arrested.'

'Shit,' I said. 'Where are you?'

'They bailed me. I'm in Aldgate.'

'What charge?'

'So far, perversion of the course of justice.'

'Not murder.'

'Not yet.'

'Bugger Oxford,' I said. 'We have to meet. Now.'

'OK. Where?'

I switched on a light and looked at my watch. Like I said, six in the morning. 'Go to Canary Wharf,' I said. 'You're close. Early risers there, or they used to be. There'll be some cafés open at this time. Find one, get some coffee and bell me. I'll be in a cab. Give me an hour.'

'OK Dad, and thanks.'

I rushed a wash, got dressed in my leather jacket and jeans and headed out. There were cabs on the rank outside, but I turned round and headed up Park Lane. At Marble Arch I hailed a blackie and we shot off east. I had my loaded Colt in my trousers – you never know who you're going to meet on a Monday morning.

Halfway there I got a call and Judith told me where she was. A little coffee shop close to Marks & Sparks. I told her I'd be there directly.

I found the place with a bit of trouble. As I'd seen from the window of the plane, the place had expanded fast since I'd skipped town, with a tube station that hadn't existed when I'd left. Nor had the branch of Marks & Spencers for that matter. At close to seven in the morning the place was already buzzing and I felt anonymous as I battled the early morning crowds, even though I was hardly dressed for business. At least, the kind of business these faceless suits understood.

Judith was sitting in the back of the café, staring into an empty coffee cup. I got one for myself. Large cappuccino. 'How you doing?' I asked when I sat down. Stupid question.

'Crap.'

'Now you've been nicked they can search your place,' I said.

'Already in hand. Probably finished by now.'

'Anything worth finding?'

'Like what?' There was fire in her eyes. That was good.

'Weapons, stolen property. Soft porn. Christ, I don't know.'

'No Dad. I'm not you. But you can bet my knicker drawers had a good going over. Always nice to know what the boss might be wearing underneath.'

'But you're not the boss at the moment.'

'Whatever.'

'Right. Tell me more about the geezer who died.'

'You know his name. Tommy Campbell. Little Scrote. Nicked him for receiving. He'd been at it for years. Recruited him as an informant. Simple.'

'A pro,' I said.

'Career criminal.'

'Right. where'd he live?'

She gave me an address in Holloway.

'Time for a visit, I think,' I said.

'The place has been searched Dad. He *was* killed there.'

I shrugged and drank some coffee. 'There's always room for a fresh pair of eyes. And I'm starving. Fancy a bacon sandwich?'

16

Judith wanted to drive me to Holloway, but I said no. 'The less we're together the better,' I said. Anyway, there were things I needed.

On the way out of Canary Wharf I found an upmarket gent's outfitter catering to the business set. It had just exactly what I wanted. A leather hat, sheepskin-lined, with ear flaps that fastened under the chin – I was fed up with the biting London wind. I caught the tube, and changed once to get to Holloway Road. In a newsagent next to the station I bought an A-Z to find the address of the flat, and on the way I struck lucky again. On the main drag there was an old fashioned ironmongers. Just the job. Maybe the gods were looking down on me and smiling. I purchased four items in the shop. A short crowbar painted black with a red tip, a length of thin metal that would work as a slim jim, a heavy screwdriver with a flat blade and one other thing. I didn't know if I'd need it – but it's better to be safe than sorry I've discovered.

It was raining when I left the shop, which was also a good sign. Keep the streets clear and keep me anonymous. I pulled up the hood of my sweatshirt over the hat and followed the directions I found in the map book.

The address was a small block of what once had been council flats, but now had a couple of For Sale notices outside. The building sat back behind a short tarmac drive with a low brick wall in front. The street itself was lined with trees, and the pedestrian traffic was light. Schools were on holiday, and by the time I got there most people had left for work, with some kids playing on the scrubby bit of grass outside the flats. The front door had been fitted with locks and a key pad, so I lit a cigarette, stood under a tree opposite and waited for someone to enter or leave. Fifteen minutes later a young mum appeared on the other side of the door with a buggy and started to struggle to get it and herself out. I was over the road smartish and held the door for her. 'Bit of work for Thompson's,' I said holding up the bag of tools. Thompson's was the name of one of the agents on the boards. I just hoped it wasn't her flat they were selling.

Obviously not, as she smiled distractedly as junior let out a howl. I slipped though the open door and watched as she walked down the drive without a backward glance. Campbell's flat was on the first floor of three. There was yellow crime scene tape covering the door. I tried my slim jim, but the door had been double locked. Shit, I thought. Here goes nothing, and I slammed the heel of my right shoe between the keyholes at the door's weakest point. The sound echoed down the corridor, but the door gave a little. One more kick and it burst open. I listened, but no one seemed interested in what I was doing so in I went, door closed behind me.

It was a small flat. One bedroom, bath/toilet, kitchen and living room. Every surface was covered with fingerprint powder and there was a nasty, dark brown stain on the living room carpet with blood splatter up one wall. Shot in the head just like Judith had told me. There was a rotten smell in the dead, cold air and I shivered involuntarily.

The place had certainly been turned over, but even experts missed things, as I knew very well. Like Judith had intimated, I'd always had something to hide in the old days and knew my business. I pulled up the edge of the carpet. Concrete floors, so no floorboards to tear up. The stereo had been pulled apart, same for the TV. The radiator in the room was solidly attached to the wall with no give. I went into the bedroom. The bed had been tipped over and the mattress was bare. On the floor was a pile of magazines. I flicked through them. All contained pictures of young men in provocative poses. Campbell was gay. Interesting. Judith hadn't mentioned that.

I checked the built-in wardrobe. Clothes on the floor, and when I tapped the back it was solid.

Next, the kitchen. The fridge was empty, doors open and pulled out from the wall. Freezer drawer as well. Too obvious. Every cop show in the world had stuff in the freezer. The oven and grill were empty too, and solid at the back. Next I went under the sink. The usual clutter, then I saw the stop cock for the water. It was black with corrosion, but when I tried it, it turned smoothly. Gotcha, I thought. Even with concrete floors you wouldn't want to flood the place. I turned it tight, then ran the water in the sink until it slowed to a few drips and headed for the bathroom. The painted plywood panel round the bath had been tugged off, and when I got down there was nothing underneath. The lid of the cistern had been removed and left on top of the toilet bowl, but when I put the crowbar behind the cistern it popped out smoothly about ten inches supported by the pipe. At the back were a couple of loose bricks, and behind them a neat little hidey hole. Inside were four plastic bags being used to keep the contents from the damp. I pulled them out. Bag one contained a little .22 revolver fully loaded. Bag two, six more bullets. Bag three, a pile of bank notes. A couple of grand I reckoned. Bag four, a little silver piece of plastic with some kind of electrical fitting at one end. It was a mystery to me, but I was sure Judith would know what it was.

I put the stuff in the carrier bag I'd got from the hardware shop, replaced the bricks and pushed the cistern back and made to leave, until I noticed something out of the corner of my eye. A flash of colour against the wall. I went to the living room window and peered out, just in time to see a police squad car pull up on the drive, blues going but no siren, and two coppers visible behind the windscreen wipers. Shit, I thought. Someone *had* heard me. I wasn't really surprised. I had made myself pretty much at home after all. I went into the bedroom and looked over the back of the flats. There was a small car park with a couple of motors on the hard standing. No sign of life though. Not even a pussy cat looking for love in the drizzle.

I pushed open the hinged window and stuck my head out. There was a drainpipe a couple of feet away, so I hung the bag of swag on my wrist, and swung myself over. With what I had bought from the hardware shop I was certainly going prepared. And what with everything else, going prepared for a long prison sentence I reckoned. Christ, I was getting too old for this lark.

I pulled myself over and hung for a second. The paint was thick and old and dried to sharp edges and I was glad I was wearing gloves, otherwise I'd have taken the skin off my hands. Then as the pipe took my full weight, I heard as much as saw the bolts attaching it to the wall start to pull free. Thank Christ it wasn't a tower block. I shimmied down as fast as I could manage, and dropped the last few feet, brushed myself off and headed for the front of the flats. I peered round the corner of the building just in time to see the front door slam behind the cops. Someone had let them in. I walked close to the wall and away, strolling back towards the main road in the rain to try and find a cab, with what Tommy Campbell had needed to keep secret even after his death I wondered who he'd been and why someone had wanted him dead.

PART 2

17

Tommy Campbell had never been a big man. A bit of a runt really, which had upset his father – who *had* been a big man. A big, violent man, who liked to get a bit fisty with Tommy's mum and Tommy himself. Tommy had never been a brave man either. But he'd been slippery all his life. Had to have been with a father like his. Learnt early when to keep out of sight. Vanish into the crowd. Not to be noticed. It had saved him a lot of grief, and had been invaluable in his career as a D-List criminal. The bravest thing he'd ever done was to have come out to his mother and father when he was eighteen. Stupidest too, as his father had gone into one and chucked Tommy out of their flat, and chucked his possessions after him. Tommy didn't bother to pick them up. He'd never gone back. Didn't know if his mum and dad were still living there, or indeed if they were living or dead. Didn't care either. Waste of space, both of them. In fact he'd enjoyed the looks on their faces when he told them he was gay. Gay, that was a laugh for a teenager on a tough estate in Leytonstone in the nineteen eighties. But, like everywhere else he'd lived since, there was a gay underground. Nods and winks. Music, clothes, pubs. Not that it was so necessary in the new millennium, but there was still prejudice, even though half the people he read about in the red-tops were as gay as tangerines these days. And those that weren't, wanted to look like they were.

So when Tommy hit the bricks all those years ago, with only the clothes he stood up in and a few quid in his bin, he'd had to fend for himself in the big bad outside world, and being slippery was his main talent.

He'd started off doing a bit of hoisting from shops in the West End. He needed somewhere as a headquarters, and for that he needed cash. No problem. He went up to Soho and got a place in a shelter for kids on the street. It was rough. A dormitory where you slept with most of your clothes on, shoes stashed under the thin pillow so they wouldn't get nicked and toilet roll stolen from boozers in your pocket, so you could at least wipe your arse.

Tommy put himself about the local pubs, chatting up likely looking marks and offering them bargains from Oxford Street and Knightsbridge to order. Simple. What did their hearts desire? A designer jacket from Harrods, denims from Selfridges, a tailored shirt from Jermyn

Street. Half price, next day delivery, and no questions asked. Sometimes there was a little hole where the shop's alarm had been cut out, but that was why the gear was so cheap.

Also, Tommy, being who he was, found that gentlemen of a certain age and disposition were happy to part with cash for certain services. Small, he was and pretty, with his tinted hair and smart clothes. And he could look younger than his age, if that was what they wanted. Because even though Tommy was living from hand to mouth, the sort of profession he was in demanded that he looked the part.

Sometimes, the gentlemen could get a bit rough. They reminded him of his father, so Tommy learned to cut up rough himself. He still wasn't brave, but the sight of a razor sharp flick knife next to the genitals often sorted out any ultra-violence towards Tommy.

As his new bank account grew, so Tommy found he could afford to move up to smarter digs. First of all a room in Fitzrovia, then a flat over a shop in a back street in Holborn. Not the Ritz, but decent enough. Tommy kept the place nice – and he could afford to buy toilet roll now.

Over the years that followed, Tommy tuned into a regular little Fagin. He met boys on the rent circuit who picked up bits and pieces as they went, and Tommy would sit warm and comfortable in his flat, buying stuff in, then selling it on. More profitable than doing the nicking himself – and safer too.

But things change, as they always do.

18

Things began to get too hot for Tommy in the West End towards the end of the nineties.

He'd managed to stay under the radar for years by constantly moving about. He never forgot walking away from his mum and dad's flat with nothing but what he stood up in, and could dump a residence in minutes. What did he need anyway? Just a bed, a chair, a decent TV, video and stereo system and some CDs. Easy to replace. Better than doing time any day. Over the years he'd moved from Holborn to King's Cross, to Euston, Covent Garden, and what was his favourite, the bottom end of Edgware Road, close to Hyde Park, where the Arabs had made the area their own. He enjoyed their culture. There was plenty of homo eroticism amongst the men, both married and single, but Tommy had become less and less interested in sex, after all the Johns he'd serviced when he first left home. Instead it was the cuisine, and the long sessions drinking thick, black, sweet coffee, and eating sugared pastries in cafes, listening to strange music, and hearing strange languages that Tommy enjoyed most.

But word was out. The traders in Oxford Street, Knightsbridge and Mayfair were becoming increasingly angry at the amount of high end goods that were going missing, and they were putting pressure on the police – who in turn were putting pressure on the courts – to come down heavily on the culprits. Gone were the days when a kid was captured by a store detective, passed on to the cops, taken away in a van, only to be immediately released and back at the hoist with half an hour. And when he or she appeared in court was just given a slap on the wrist, and fine that could be paid for with less than an hour's shoplifting.

Even someone as careful as Tommy Campbell knew that his clean sheet couldn't last forever, and when it was time to fold up his tent and do a vanishing act.

So Tommy relocated to south London – but not too far south. Waterloo was just a couple of miles from his old hunting grounds, but a world away socially and economically.

Tommy sub-let a council flat in a block in The Cut, close to the Old Vic, for a chunk of key money. One bedroom on the seventh floor, with a view across to the Elephant and Castle. This time he'd brought his necessities and was soon settled in. But of course he

needed dough to live. The rent boys were left behind, but
he soon found replacements. Young mums from the
Aylesbury, the North Peckham, and the other, smaller
estates between Waterloo and London Bridge.

The girls were single, living with their kids in council
flats, claiming benefits, and making money where and
when they could. Even though they were on their own,
there was no shortage of men, hence the growing number
of illegitimate children in the area.

Tommy met the first of new recruits in the Cut Market
where he was buying fruit and veg one Saturday
afternoon. 'You'll get stuff free later when they close,'
said a chubby blonde teenager pushing a baby buggy.

'Do what?' he replied.

'When they pack up, they leave all sorts of stuff lying
about,' she explained. 'Everything. It's not worth them
keeping it 'til Monday, so you can have a good scrounge.'

'I never knew,' he said.

'Not local?'

'Just moved in last week.'

'You'll learn. Fancy a cuppa?'

There was a Wimpy bar a few yards away, and they went
in and ordered two teas and an orange squash for the baby,
which she decanted into his bottle. 'Jack,' she said,
indicating the infant who was sucking on the bottle's teat
like a fiend. 'And I'm Sandra.'

'Tommy,' said Tommy. 'Pleased to meet you.'

'You looked a bit lost,' she said, lighting a Benson and
Hedges.

'I am I suppose. More used to the other side of the river.'

'It's all right round here once you get used to it,' she said. 'So, you on the dole?'

'Self employed,' he replied, enjoying the conversation and the company. He was so used to being on his own, it didn't often happen.

'Doing what?'

'Hoisting and flogging gear, as it goes,' he said, deciding to tell the truth. If she didn't like it, he'd leave. He couldn't read her expression, but then she replied,

'Blimey. I thought I recognised a mate when I saw you. Me too. Me and a few of my pals.'

'Sweet,' said Tommy. 'Where d'you get rid of the stuff?'

'Anywhere we can.'

'You should get organised.'

'It's the kids see. Hard to do the bizzo when they're around.'

'I'll sort you if you like,' said Tommy. 'That's my game.'

'You reckon.'

'Trust me, I've done it for years up west, but things started to get a bit sticky.'

'OK, Tommy. I'll think about it. Got a mobile?'

'Yeah.'

'Give us the number and I'll bell you.'

Tommy wrote his phone number on the back of a paper napkin, and handed it over.

'Cheers,' said Sandra. 'You got a bird?'

'No,' said Tommy.

'Thought not. You got a bloke?'

'You're sharp,' said Tommy.

'Got to be round here,' she said, cheekily.

Tommy grinned, finished his tea, and left the cafe. Just like Sandra had said, there was fruit and vegetables in boxes all along the kerb, and people were picking though them. Tommy spotted a cauliflower with just a few black marks on the florets and popped it into his carrier bag. He waved to Sandra as he walked back past the Wimpy and she indicated that she would phone him, making the universal sign with her hand next to her ear. He gave her a thumbs up in reply.

Result, he thought, as he made the short walk back to the flat.

On the following Monday morning, around ten thirty, Tommy was sitting in front of the TV watching *This Morning* and eating his breakfast of toast, jam and tea, when his mobile buzzed. He didn't recognise the number, but answered. 'Tommy, it's Sandra. Remember me?'

'Course I do. What can I do for you?'

'We should make a meet.'

'All right. When?'

'Soon as.'

Tommy was careful about giving his address to someone he had just met, but he had spent most of Sunday exploring the area and had a plan. 'There's a park behind the Old Vic. With swings and things. Know it?'

'Course.'

'It's a nice morning. How about we meet there? Jack can go on the roundabout.'

'All right. See you there. What, say half an hour?'

'Sounds OK to me,' said Tommy. 'See ya.' And he turned off the phone.

He finished his breakfast, washed up the few crocks and headed across The Cut to the park, stopping to get a paper in the corner newsagent on the way. The park was empty when he got there, it being a school day, and he sat on a bench, lit a cigarette and read the headlines. The sun was warm, and the back street outside was quiet, and all in all Tommy decided he'd made a good choice of his new location.

Ten minutes later, Sandra walked down the street pushing Jack in his buggy. She was accompanied by a coffee coloured girl with her hair in braids, also pushing a pram. The pair joined Tommy on the bench. 'Hello Tom,' said Sandra. 'This is my mate Shaz.'

'Hello Shaz,' said Tommy.

'Hello,' replied the girl 'Nice to meetcha.'

'I've had a few words with the girls,' said Sandra. 'And we want to give what you said a go. What's the deal?'

'You hoist the stuff and bring it to me,' said Tommy. 'I make contacts round and about, and flog the gear on at half the marked price. Then we split the dough fifty fifty. I used to do well up town, but like I told you, things got a bit iffy. So let's not crowd the market first off. What sort of gear you talking about anyway?'

'Anything fits up our skirts, or in the buggy with the kids,' said Sandra. 'Stuff for the home mostly. But we can get clothes. Women's stuff usually, obviously. But if you get an order we'll do our best to fill it.'

Tommy was too much of a gentleman to mention that Sandra and Shaz's skirts were so short, he didn't think they'd get much gear up them. 'Where do you get the stuff?' he asked.

'Croydon, Clapham, or we sometimes all pile into a motor and do the shopping centres in Essex and Kent.'

'An awayday,' said Tommy, smiling.

'You got it.'

And so the deal was made.

And over the next year or so, Tommy had no regrets.

Sandra and Shaz had a lot of mates, and they were most enthusiastic hoisters. Tommy rented a secure lockup close to his block that soon resembled Aladdin's cave. The girls nicked anything that wasn't nailed down. Sheets, duvets, kitchenware, radios, videos, CD players, CDs, children's clothes, anything. They went out mob handed, keeping in touch by the mobile phones that were gradually getting more popular. They kept an eye out for store detectives, and occasionally there was a bit of fisticuffs if one got too close, but on the whole they kept the violence to a minimum. Business was slow at first, as Tommy had predicted, but it picked up fast when he began to be known around the local cafés and pubs. The money rolled in. Every couple of days, he'd host what he called his 'coffee mornings' when the girls would come to his flat, dump the babies in the bedroom under the eye of a little sister and in a fug of cigarette smoke, show Tommy their swag, and collect their earnings.

He'd never in his life been happier. He had a family again.

After the business was done, someone would go down The Cut and bring back a takeaway from one of the many restaurants in the market. After lunch, the girls would break out the joints and everyone got happily stoned and had a good old gossip.

Although the young women were officially on their own, there was no shortage of blokes about. Boyfriends, brothers, brothers-in-law, uncles and dads. And most of them on the rob in some way or another. And what tales of villainy Tommy heard on those afternoons, surrounded by marijuana smoke. All sorts of dirty deeds done cheap, and sometimes not so cheap at that. Burglaries, armed robberies, drug deals, pimping. All sorts. He loved to listen, and when things went properly pear-shaped for him at the beginning of the new millennium, he discovered not only a way to slide out of trouble, but also a lucrative sideline. It ended up being his main source of income.

19

The beginning of Tommy's downfall started out as just another day.

After almost two years on the manor, he had become a well known fixture. The market-stall holders always gave him a cheery greeting. They, along with the local publicans, took advantage of his cheap gear, and he considered himself fireproof. The girls came and went, but there were always new recruits to be found, and Tommy made a fair living. Not extravagant, but then he was happy with the way things were.

But once again, things were about to change.

It all started one Saturday with Tommy in one of his locals on the Blackfriars Road, having a pie and chips washed down with a pint of Guinness. A well-dressed young couple came in, bought drinks, sat at the next table and began discussing the house they'd renovated in one of the turnings off Union Street. Recently there'd been an influx of what Tommy still considered to be Yuppies, buying up old properties in the newly-gentrified Borough and Waterloo areas, which were now considered property hot spots. Tommy had done business with lots of them on recommendation, and was always looking for new customers for his little empire. He listened hard as the woman complained about the price of a range of French cookware she wanted, and Tommy leant over and said, 'maybe I can help you.'

The couple looked at him in surprise.

'Sorry,' he said. 'But I couldn't help overhearing.'

'Oh, my wish list,' said the young woman. 'It's a bore, but we're so over budget on the house.'

'I know,' said Tommy. 'It's a joke. But I might be able to pick up some of that stuff. Le Creuset, right?'

'You know about kitchenware,' said the young bloke.

'My line,' said Tommy, smiling disarmingly.

'And you can source it,' said the woman.

'Could take a week or so,' said Tommy, who did indeed know about kitchenware, and the few shops that carried that top of the line range. 'Volcanic orange, I take it?'

Tommy's new friends beamed at him. 'How much?' asked the man.

'Half retail price to new customers,' said Tommy.

'You're joking,' said the woman. 'How can you... ?' She looked sceptical.

'Don't ask questions,' said the man.

Tommy smiled again. 'It's not a problem. Cut out the middle man. Easy really. Low overheads.'

'Enough said,' said the man. 'Can we get you a drink?'

'No thanks,' said Tommy. 'Must dash. Got a number I can reach you on?'

The man supplied a mobile number. 'I'll bell you next week,' said Tommy. 'It weighs a bit this stuff, so you'll have to collect.'

'Our pleasure,' said the man. 'My name's Steve by the way, and this is Delia.'

'Nice to meet you,' said Tommy. 'Anyway, I'll shoot off and see what I can see.'

'Do you need some sort of deposit?' asked the man, looking hopeful.

'No,' said Tommy. 'I could be on the con. That's not the way I do business. Ask anyone round here. If I can get the stuff, which I'm sure I can, it'll be cash on delivery. Otherwise... Well, let's just see what happens.'

'I'll wait for your call Tommy,' said Steve, 'And thanks. That stuff costs an arm and a leg in John Lewis.'

'No problem,' he replied, as he drained his glass and left.

Tommy didn't know it yet, but it was the beginning of the end.

Although some of Tommy's girls had come and gone, Sandra and Shaz were still with him, and still the most dedicated of shoplifters. When he got back from the pub that lunchtime he gave Sandra a call. 'Got an order,' he said when she answered.

'What?' she asked.

'Pop round and I'll tell you.' He still didn't like doing business on the phone.

She turned up an hour later. 'What?' she asked when she was sitting down with a cup of tea. Her skirts were longer now, and she was chubbier, but that was because there was another little Sandra on the way. Husband unknown. 'It might be Geoff,' she said. 'Or it might be Terry. Or it might be someone I met down the boozer one night. Tommy, you know what I'm like when I've had a lager or two.'

Tommy knew, then he explained what was wanted.

'Christ,' she said. 'That stuff weighs a ton.'

'You've got time. And take Shaz with you.'

'I dunno about that,' she said. 'She's had a result.'

What? Asked Tommy.

'You know her new bloke Jacko.'

'Sort of.'

'You know about that bank truck that got robbed in Nunhead the other week?'

'Yeah.'

'He drove one of the motors in the job.'

'Get away.'

'Yeah. One of the getaway drivers.'

'Blimey.'

'So Shaz has got a few bob for once.'

'Come on Sandra,' he said. 'It's good money.'

'All right Tommy, I'll see what she says.'

Sandra must have convinced her, because the next day

she phoned him again. 'You're on,' she said.

In fact the full set of kitchenware was delivered by pram by Thursday afternoon, and Tommy phoned Steve's mobile. 'Got your stuff,' he said. 'Let's make a meet.'

'I'm off tomorrow,' said Steve. 'In the pub, twelevish.'

'Sweet,' said Tommy. 'Bring the dough like we said.'

'Course,' said Steve.

They met up at noon the next day. Steve had a bundle of cash in his pocket. 'Listen,' he said 'I can't stop, can we get the stuff now. My car's outside.'

Tommy gulped down his drink and they left the pub, went to Steve's car, and Tommy directed him to his block. 'It's boxed up,' he said. 'You wait here, I'll get the stuff and we'll do the biz.'

'Sounds good,' said Steve, and Tommy went up to his flat, hefted up the heavy carton, and went back downstairs.

He put the box on the front passenger seat and opened it. 'A full set,' he said.

'Terrific,' said Steve, who got out of the car and walked round to Tommy's side. 'Thomas Campbell,' he said, showing him a police warrant card, and introducing himself as Detective Constable Steven Wells. 'I'm arresting you for handling stolen goods.' He told him his rights, and showed him warrants to search his flat and lock up.

'Do what,' said Tommy. 'You can't. This is entrapment.'

'No mate,' said Steve. 'You introduced yourself and made the offer. It's all down on tape.'

He took a police radio from the pocket of his coat, and said, 'Control. It's 531. Let's have the backup round to Campbell's flat. He's all ready for interview.'

Tommy couldn't believe his bad luck. All this time with a clean sheet, then he had an idea. 'Here listen,' he said. 'I might have something for you. That truck that got hijacked last week in Nunhead. I know something about it.'

'If you're lying...,' said Steve.

'Straight up,' said Tommy. 'Can't we do some sort of deal?'

'Might do,' said Steve.

So, as one door closed, another opened.

Tommy never looked back.

20

Steve bundled Tommy into his car and drove to the local nick where he was banged up in a cell after giving his details to the custody sergeant and being parted with the few belongings he carried.

Twenty minutes later the woman who'd been introduced as Delia came to his cell. 'Tommy,' she said. 'I'm Detective Sergeant Judith Sharman. This little job is my responsibility. Now my DC tells me you have some information that might be useful.'

'Yeah,' said Tommy. 'But I want a deal.'

'You know we don't do deals Tommy.'

'Like hell you don't.'

'OK. Let's go and have a little chat.'

They went to an interview room where they were joined by Steve. There was a recording device in the room, but

DS Sharman left it turned off. 'OK, Tommy,' she said. 'What do you know?'

'I know the name of one of the getaway drivers done that job in Nunhead last week, where that money truck got hijacked. I know where his bird lives, and I know that he spends a lot of time round there with her.'

Sharman looked at Steve. 'What do you reckon?' she said.

'I know he's smart enough to have a clean record, though I reckon he's been at it for years. And I know he's supposed to be mates with every toe rag in the area. I know that from watching him for weeks. And I know that nicking that gang could get us both promoted. Better than pulling some small time bunch of thieves nicking bloody pots and pans, anyway.'

'My DC was never over enamoured with this job,' said Judith. 'OK, Tommy. We forget about our little sting and you spill the beans. You've not been formally charged, so there's no paperwork. But I warn you. If you're taking the piss I'll make sure you regret it big time.'

'It's the truth,' said Tommy. 'I swear.'

He supplied the cops with Shaz's name and address, and the name of her new boyfriend, and an hour later he was back on the bricks, still with a clean record. But he also knew that if anyone sussed out what he'd done he was as good as dead.

21

Tommy heard about Shaz's flat being busted through the Waterloo grapevine. It was the talk of the Cut market, where Shaz did her shopping, and drank in the pubs. Her new boyfriend, Jacko had been nicked for armed robbery and conspiracy, and was on remand in Brixton. She was down the local nick as an accessory, and gave up some names. Grass, was the word round the stalls and cafés and boozers between Waterloo Road and Westminster Bridge Road. Grass. Tommy began to feel safe until he got a call from Sandra. 'You didn't say nothing did you Tom?' she asked. 'What I told you about Jacko. It's all gone tits up.'

'Course not.'

'Cos someone told me you were spotted with one of the filth what nicked him.'

'No.'

'You better not have mate. There's some very nasty people out there looking for someone to give a spank to. Shaz is in the frame, but I know better. She'd never talk to coppers. Anyway, she was having too good a time on Jacko's wedge. So just watch out Tom. You never know who's whispering names for a drink.'

'It weren't me, honest,' said Tommy. But inside he knew it was time to make a move. He'd miss the manor, but that was too bad. He'd miss his neck more.

He packed a small holdall with everything he needed, took one last look round his flat at all the stuff he'd have to leave behind, but at least he had his freedom, and was just opening the front door when a man's voice said. 'Hello Tommy. Taking a trip?'

He nearly passed out until he recognised Steve and DS Sharman standing on his landing. 'Christ,' he said. 'Don't do that.'

'Holiday?' said Judith.

'No. I'm off, thanks to you. There's whispers around about me, and I don't need the ag.'

'You done well Tommy,' said Steve. 'Very well.'

'Lost my living though.'

'You'll survive,' said Judith. 'We're both up for promotion on the strength of your intel, and I'm being transferred up West.'

'Congratulations,' said Tommy.

'Listen. Where you off to?'

'Dunno. North London somewhere. As far away as I can

from here and still be in the smoke.'

Judith took a card out of her handbag and wrote a number on the back. 'My mobile,' she said. 'You hear anything like the last lot wherever you are and call me. There'll be a few quid in it for you.'

Tommy took the card and stuck it in his pocket. 'I'll think about it,' he said.

'You do that.'

They both watched as Tommy took the stairs down to the street and vanished in the direction of Waterloo Station. 'What do you reckon sarge?' asked Steve.

'He'll be in touch,' said Judith. 'Sure as you're born.'

And she was right.

22

That first day, Tommy got a room in an Irish house in West Hampstead from a card in a newsagent's window. It was a bit of a khazi, but the bloke who ran the place was an old Nancy-boy and made Tommy a decent cup of tea, the sheets were clean enough, and although it was a shared bathroom, Tommy's room had a washbasin so at least he could have a piss in private. And the area was well served with cheap eating places.

'Staying long?' asked the landlord over the cuppa.

''Til the money runs out,' replied Tommy. It was the truth, and there wasn't much of it about. He thought of all the expensive gear he'd abandoned in Waterloo, but just shrugged again. Having all his limbs intact was worth more than a few fancy Japanese electrical goods.

He settled down in the cafés and pubs like always, but

his heart was no longer in the hoisting game. He'd lost his crew, and wasn't in the mood to find another. There'd never be anyone like Sandra and her pals and he knew it. Tommy was running out of options. Hoisting was the only job he'd ever had; he couldn't see himself signing on the dole at his age. He often looked at the copper's card, and decided that being an informant might be the way to go. But that wasn't as easy as it was the first time.

He trawled the pubs, clubs and cafés of the area, taking in Kilburn, Cricklewood and Camden but no luck. Then he had a lucky break. The landlord told him that the bloke who ran a snooker and pool hall nearby was looking for a pot man to clear the tables, wash the glasses and fetch and carry for the clientele – who were the epitome of low life. 'Cash in hand Tommy,' he said. 'I know you could use a shilling or two. I've put a word in for you.'

So Tommy, who had never had a proper job in his life, ended up getting cigarettes and hot pies for the members of the club, clearing up after them, and eavesdropping on their conversations.

It was like he was invisible all over again, and he heard all sorts from the punters, their various ethnicities making the club resemble a United Nations of the criminal world, but it was mostly small time crime. He knew that if he was going to earn from the copper, he'd need to bring her something big. He needed enough for a deposit on a decent place to live, and to replace some of the stuff he'd lost.

Then one day it dropped into his lap.

It seemed that over in Shepherd's Bush, a pair of Pakistani brothers ran a cash and carry warehouse off the Goldhawk Road, catering for the local corner shops. A lot of cash. And the brothers had a profitable sideline – laundering money for various individuals, including a Balkan gang based in Notting Hill. But the Pakistani guys were big time gamblers – and big time losers. They'd lost some of the gang's loot and seemed to be in no hurry to replace it.

Now, the brothers took part in a very high-stakes poker game every Friday night at their warehouse. It tended to last through most of the weekend. The buy-in was twenty-thousand pounds, and there were often half a dozen players at any one time. A lot of money and only one minder to keep the peace.

Tommy overheard two of the Balkans who often dropped in for a game of pool discussing the game, and the plan to knock it over the following Saturday evening. The brothers' names, the address, everything. Everything he needed to earn a big cash payout from the police.

On his next run for supplies Tommy phoned DS Sharman on his new mobile.

'It's been a long time, Tommy,' she said.

'Not so long,' he replied.

'You got something for me?'

'Oh yes.'

'Something good?'

'Oh yes.'

'Then let's make a meet. And by the way, it's Detective-

Inspector now, thanks to you.'

They met shortly afterwards in a pub in Bayswater. Tommy told her the gist of his information, but kept the names and location to himself. He intended to keep something back for bargaining purposes.

'Sounds good,' said Judith. 'If it's kosher.'

'It's kosher all right,' said Tommy. 'These bastards don't mess about. I've heard stories...'

'Save them for another day,' interrupted Judith. 'It's Saturday that interests me. How much?'

'For a grand I'll tell you the full monty.'

'I bet you will Tommy. But a grand's a lot just on your say so. I don't even know where you're living these days. You might just vanish into the mystic, like you did when you left your last abode.'

'That's why I need at least a grand,' said Tommy. 'I'm running low on readies. Christ, I'm grafting for pennies at the moment. I need a base. Somewhere where I don't have to take my own shit paper to the lavatory with me in my pocket.'

'Too much information Tommy,' said Judith. 'All right, I'll put you on the books as an official informant. *If* the intel is right.'

'A grand?' said Tommy.

'A grand it is. But not until after Saturday, and all the bad men are in the cells.'

'Fair enough,' said Tommy. 'I'll have to trust you I suppose.'

'Trust is a two way street Tommy,' she said. 'If I round

up a team from the local nick, wherever it is, and it goes pear shaped, I'll never live it down. For all I know, you could be winding me up for what happened before.'

'I swear,' said Tommy.

'OK. Spill the beans. Where's this job going off?'

Tommy told her the names of the brothers and the address of the cash and carry, keeping his voice low, and she vanished outside with her mobile phone stuck to her ear.

When she came back, she said, 'They're in the system,' she said. 'Shepherd's Bush superintendent just about wet his knickers. Looks like we're on.'

'The money?' asked Tommy.

'Next week, son,' said Judith. 'Bell me on Sunday.'

The robbery went down in the small hours of Sunday morning. DI Sharman had been part of an armed team keeping obbo on the warehouse, and had been on tenterhooks as the hours passed and no one showed. But, the police officers' patience was eventually rewarded, and a load of bodies were nicked – not only the Balkans, who had arrived with plenty of firepower, but also the Pakistani brothers, who had some very interesting paperwork in the offices referring to certain illegal activities.

Tommy heard all about it on the little portable radio at six am. The raid had ended in a shootout which had closed half of Shepherd's Bush. Thank fuck, he thought. Now maybe I can get out of this shit hole.

23

And so Tommy Campbell became DI Judith Sharman's main source of intelligence, which worked out well for both of them. Tommy picked up plenty of gossip at the snooker hall, and at the Irish house where he still kept a room, but he'd moved on to a small flat in Holloway. No one knew him except a young man named Cedric who he met at the local kebab shop, and who became his lover, his first for many years.

Life was ticking along nicely until the day Tommy was strolling to the tube, only to see an anonymous, dark-coloured saloon with tinted windows pulling up ahead of him. Two men got out of the back and walked towards him. For once Tommy's radar was on the blink. They gathered him up without fuss and put him in the car between the two of them. The driver pulled away almost before Tommy realised what had happened. 'What?' was all he managed to say in a strangled tone.

'Shut up,' said the elder of the two men. 'Or you'll be sorry.'

Tommy did as he was told, but he felt like the bottom had fallen out of his stomach – and his whole world for that matter.

The car drove up towards Archway then turned in the direction of Muswell Hill before pulling into a leafy side road and stopping. The driver got out of the car and lit a cigarette whilst the older man told Tommy exactly what was going to happen. 'You've been telling tales, haven't you Tommy?' he said.

'Dunno what you mean,' said Tommy, his heart going a mile a minute.

'Don't worry,' said the man. 'We're not going to hurt you. We just know about your relationship with DI Sharman.'

'You Old Bill?' said Tommy.

'Now if we were, we'd have to respect PACE, and your rights to legal representation. No. We work directly for Her Majesty. We do what the police can't. And because of your unique position, you're going to work directly for Her Majesty too.'

Tommy began to feel better. 'What about the DI?' he asked.

'What the DI doesn't know won't hurt her,' said the man. 'And we wouldn't want her hurt would we?'

Tommy shook his head. Not as long as she's holding

cash, he thought. 'What's in it for me?' he asked.

'Money, and Her Majesty's eternal gratitude, of course,' he smirked.

Tommy couldn't care less what Her Majesty thought. 'So what do I do?'

'There's a pair of Russian brothers use your place of employment. Georgie and Alexie. Know who I mean?'

Tommy knew only too well. A right pair of arscholes was his estimate of them. Always off their heads on coke, vodka and champagne, which they sent him out to buy from the local offie. Lousy pool players too, who always wanted to bet on the games, and always lost. But they were dangerous, despite outward appearances. Very, very scary with it. 'I know them,' he said.

'They're running a scam in conjunction with their mother. Blackmail. We don't like it. We want hard evidence. You can get it for us.'

'How?'

'Earn your money Tommy,' said the man. 'You work it out.'

'They're hard men,' said Tommy, already feeling fearful.

The man sighed, reached into his pocket and Tommy cringed. 'Relax,' he said, and pulled out an envelope. 'Five grand Tommy,' he said. 'Now, do you think you can work something out?'

Tommy reached for the envelope, the lure of the money overriding his instincts to cut his losses, get out now. 'Sure,' he said. 'I'm sure I can.'

The man pulled the envelope back. 'Just one other

thing,' he said. The other man picked up a briefcase from the floor and opened it, pulling out a sheaf of papers and a pen. 'Sign that,' said the older man.

'What is it?' said Tommy.

'The Official Secrets Act. You tell anyone about this meeting, or what you're doing for us, and you'll vanish off the face of the earth. *Capiche?*'

Tommy capiched, and signed the paper with an only slightly shaking hand. He pocketed the money and the older man beckoned the driver back into the car. Tommy was driven to Holloway and dropped off in front of the tube station.

'Remember what I said,' said the man as Tommy got out. 'Not a word. We'll be in touch.'

Tommy couldn't help thinking that he was entering a very bad place, but knew he had no choice but to earn his money, and succeed. He cozied up to the Russian brothers, running out to keep them topped up on liquor, complimenting them on their gaudy clothes and praising their non-existent pool and snooker skills. Soon he was collecting cocaine from their dealer, taking their laundry to the cleaners, and doing any shopping they needed. They introduced him to their mother, a vile, overweight harridan, as their 'Little Queer'. Tommy just smiled and gritted his teeth.

But as for the blackmail business, they kept Tommy well in the dark. This didn't please Tommy's contact at HMG, who identified himself only as Smith. 'Listen, you little shit,' he said. 'I've paid you good money for information, not to have you swanning around town in a taxi picking up those bastards clean underwear.'

'I'm doing my best,' complained Tommy, exasperated. 'You think I enjoy their company? They're fucking bonkers the pair of them. And as for their mother, she's a right old bag.'

'My heart bleeds,' said Smith. 'Just get on with it.'

But Tommy wasn't as clueless as he pretended. He might not have got much info on the blackmail plot so far, but he'd sussed out that the family ran a string of whores from their flat in Knightsbridge. Plus a couple of geeky looking eastern Europeans who never spoke, but were locked away in a room in the flat with a load of computer equipment.

Tommy signed his own death warrant the day he stole a memory stick from the flat.

His plan was to blackmail the blackmailers and collect a bundle of money – from the safety of a place a long way away.

But the best laid plans...

The theft was ridiculously easy. The brothers had been on a three day bender, and woke Tommy one Sunday morning with demands for more drugs. They were at home with a pair of their underage whores, so Tommy dragged himself out of bed, called a mini cab and headed for Clerkenwell where the dealer lived. He had to drag *him* out of bed, which didn't please him, but like most people, he was so frightened of the Russians that he supplied the necessary on account and returned to his pit.

Tommy headed west in the cab and the brothers, both looking like zombies, ushered him into their flat. Of their mother there was no sign, but there *was* a young half naked prostitute in the living room. She covered her bare breasts when Tommy entered. 'Don't worry sister,' said Georgie. 'You're not his type.'

Tommy just smiled.

'Make coffee,' said Georgie as he snarfed up a spoonful of cocaine from one of the wraps. 'Make yourself useful.'

Tommy went into the kitchen, which looked like a bomb had hit it. He fired up the coffee maker, washed up some cups and went back to the living room. It was empty, but from the sounds from the bedroom next door, caffeine was the last thing that was wanted.

Then Tommy noticed that the computer room door was ajar.

He sidled up and peered round the jamb. Empty. One of the computers was live, and Tommy spotted a memory stick in its fresh packaging on the table next to it. He was no computer expert, but Cedric had taught him the basics. Tommy swiftly unwrapped the stick, stuck it into its slot on the keyboard and copied what was on the machine's hard drive. It only took seconds, but Tommy almost pissed himself at the risk he was taking.

But no one came to the door, and a minute or so later Tommy was back in the kitchen trying not to think about what he had just stolen from the Russians.

And what they would do to him if they realised.

PART THREE

24

When I got back to my room in the hotel the message light was flashing on the phone. It was the desk telling me that if I wanted to stay longer I'd have to move rooms, so would I collect my stuff together so that the staff could shift it. I agreed, asked them to give me an hour, took off my sodden clothes and took a long, hot shower. Then I called Judith. 'We need to meet,' I said 'Right away.'

'You found something,' she said.

'Correct.'

We agreed on a location. A pub on the Bayswater Road at noon. I dressed myself in a suit and tie and packed my bag. It was now weighed down with two guns and ammunition, the crowbar, slim jim, screwdriver and my other purchase. But I had no choice but to leave them, and hoped that the porter who was going to move my stuff wasn't of a nosey disposition. I wrapped the metal as much as possible with fabric so it didn't clank, zipped up the bag, then got a piece of soap and carefully worked some into the zip. If it was disturbed when I got back I'd know if the bag had been opened. It wasn't much, but I couldn't trust anyone, and at least I'd be prepared for a visit from the law. I hung my damp clothes on the heated towel rail, left a twenty pound note on the pillow as a tip next to the rest of my new clothes, grabbed my overcoat, slipped into my shoes and left the room. On the way out I dropped my key card off at reception, and was told by the smiling receptionist that I could collect the one for my new room on my return. In one pocket of my coat I had the cash I'd found, in the other the plastic doodad that I'd taken from Campbell's cistern, along with the gun and money.

I cabbed through the park and found Judith waiting in the boozer. It was already starting to fill up with drinkers and we found a quiet table in the conservatory in the back. The rain was heavy again and dripped down the windows, distorting the view of the garden outside.

'What?' she said.

'You didn't tell me he was gay. Your snout.'

'Didn't think it was important.'

'Everything's important. Did he have a boyfriend?'

She shrugged. 'I don't know.'

'Could be a crime of passion.'

'Just because he was gay?'

'Just thinking aloud.'

'So what did you find?'

'Money,' I told her, and showed her the packet. I'd had time to count it back at the hotel. Two thousand eight hundred quid in used notes. More than I'd thought.

'There was a gun and ammunition too.'

'Christ. They haven't found the gun that killed him. At least not so far as I know. They hadn't when I was suspended.'

'I don't think this was the one. It was clean and fully loaded. I doubt whether a murderer would have cleaned his weapon and hidden it where this one was. And left the cash. What calibre was the gun, do you know?'

'Nine mill.'

I shook my head. 'No. This one's a baby. A twenty two.' Then I remembered. 'I found this too.' I showed her the piece of plastic.

'A memory stick,' she said.

'What?'

'It goes in a port on the side of a computer. Contains information. Didn't you know?'

'No. I've never been any good with computers. And there wasn't one at the flat.'

Dinosaur, I could see in her eyes. 'That would have been the first thing they would have taken as evidence,' she said. 'If there was one. I don't know. I wasn't privy to that information. Maybe that was one of the things they were searching for when they turned my place over.'

'Could you find out?'

'I'll try. But don't count on it.'

'But this must be important for him to stash it away. Can we get the information on it? You must have a computer.'

'Mine was taken in the search last night.'

'Shit.'

'It'll probably be password protected anyway. The stick.'

'Who'd have the password?'

'If it is, and it's the same as his computer itself, and they've broken it, the IT boys at the Yard.'

'Could you get it?'

'I'm on suspension don't forget. And Christ they'd smell a rat if I tried wouldn't they?'

'Yeah. If he had a boyfriend do you think he'd know?'

'Could do.'

'Looks like we're going to have to try and find him.'

'You're joking. Needle in a haystack. We don't even know if he had one.'

'You didn't know much about this geezer did you?'

'He was my informant. I didn't want a relationship.'

'Perhaps you should have.'

'Perhaps,' she said, a little angrily.

'We'll put that on the back burner for now. If we get a computer could we try this thing?'

'Sure.'

'Then let's buy one.'

25

We shot off in Judith's car, over Notting Hill and down towards Shepherd's Bush and White City where she found a trading estate of huge shops that seemed to sell nothing but sofas and computers. Welcome to the Twenty-first century I thought.

We parked up and ran through the rain to the shop and found a listless looking assistant playing some sort of shoot 'em up game on a giant plasma screened TV. 'We need a laptop,' said Judith.

'No problemo,' said the boy whom I immediately wanted to slap. 'We've got plenty.'

'Something that will take this,' I said, showing him the memory stick.

'Easy,' he said, smiling at Judith.

He showed us over to a bank of small computers and

started his sales pitch. 'This one'll do,' I said, pointing at a matt black machine.

'OK,' said the boy, rather disappointed that he couldn't show more of his knowledge. 'I'll get one out of stock.'

'Is it ready to go?' I asked.

'Well no sir, we'll get one of our technicians to call round to your house and load up the software, get your internet ready and...'

'No,' I interrupted. 'I don't have a house, I'm in transit, and I need it right away.'

'Well that's...'

I pulled out my wallet and fished out a fifty pound note. 'Do you know how to get it ready?' I asked.

'Of course.'

'Then do it.'

'Well that's not really...'

'And another fifty when it's done.'

'Well I suppose... It is nearly my lunch hour.'

'Go on then.'

The fifty vanished into his sky rocket. 'How long?' I asked.

'Half an hour.' But before that I had to go through his little sales pitch about an extended guarantee which I refused, then give him a room number in the Shepherd's Bush Hilton as my temporary address, and tell more lies as he passed my American Express card through his machine, before the computer belonged to me, or at least to James Stark.

'Anywhere we can get coffee?' I asked when we'd finished.

'IKEA across the road.'

So that's where we had lunch. Swedish meatballs, and that ain't no joke.

We went back and the machine was ready. 'I put some life in the battery,' the boy explained after I paid him another fifty quid. 'But you'd better put it on a long charge as soon as you can.'

'I'll do that,' I said, and we took the thing out to the car. Judith fired it up and inserted the memory stick. A little icon popped onto the screen and she clicked it with the pointer, and of course it asked for a password. 'Bugger,' she said. 'That's it then. Maybe I'd better turn this in.'

'You're joking,' I said. 'They might wonder where it came from.'

'Right,' she said. 'Wasn't thinking.'

'Someone must have an idea about the password,' I said. 'He must've had friends. Maybe a lover boy.'

'How do you suggest we find out?'

'Go back to the flats. Ask around. You're the copper.'

'On suspension. No warrant.'

'Don't you have a *doppelganger*?'

'Do what?'

'Another warrant card. Come on, I did.'

'I just bet you did.'

I gave her a look. 'I might have something...' she continued.

'Got it with you?'

She nodded.

'That's my girl. Let's go to Holloway.'

'Can't. Terms of bail. I've got to report in.'

'Shit. Tomorrow?'

She nodded again.

'Right. Call me in the morning. I know some people are at home during the day at his flats. OK?'

'OK,' she replied.

'Drop me off where I can get a cab. I'll take the computer.'

'Now don't break it,' she said.

'Don't you trust your old dad? I was doing this when you were just a twinkle in my eye,' I told her.

26

When I got back to the hotel I was shown to my new room overlooking the back of the building. My clothes had been hung up neatly, and the soap was undisturbed on the bag. I settled down with the crossword, ate a steak and chips on room service and had a good night's sleep – for a change.

Judith picked me up the next morning from a café on the north side of Oxford Street. I was back in jeans and leather, befitting one of the forces of law and order in the capital. I had my belly gun in one pocket and the other item I'd purchased in the hardware shop in Holloway in the other. I didn't show it to Judith.

'There was no computer found at Campbell's flat,' she said, as soon as we got in the car.

'Interesting,' I said. 'So they probably thought you

had it away.'

'It wasn't mentioned.'

'Why should they? If you had stolen it I doubt they thought you were going to roll over and admit it. Got a warrant card?' I asked.

She showed me a leather folder. 'It belonged to a friend,' she said.

'Don't matter,' I replied. 'No one ever looks at them anyway.'

'They do nowadays,' she said.

I wasn't sure about that, but kept quiet.

We drove down to Holloway and parked around the corner from the flats. Better to be safe than identified by a car number. She was going to be DS Smith, and I was her colleague DC Gardner. A bit ancient for a mere constable, I thought, but said nothing. She was the boss. We walked up the drive to the flats and she started pressing bells. Eventually a male voice answered. 'Police,' said Judith, the door buzzed and we were in.

'Told you,' I said.

After a minute or two a figure appeared at the top of the first flight of stairs. A bloke in jeans and sweatshirt with what hair he had left standing on end. Judith flashed the brief and said. 'Good morning. Sorry to disturb you. DS Smith. We're making follow up enquiries about Thomas Campbell. Did you know him'

'The bloke what got shot?' said the man still standing above us.

Judith nodded, I stayed quiet.

'Can't say as I did,' he said. 'Opposite end of the corridor downstairs. I'm on the top floor at the back. Never saw or heard a thing. I've already been through this, and I was trying to get to sleep. I work nights.'

'Sorry,' said Judith again.

'I suppose it don't matter,' he said. 'Night off, and I need to get to the shops. Is that it?'

'Yes,' said Judith. 'And once again, sorry to have bothered you.'

The bloke just shrugged and walked up the stairs away from us.

'Good start,' said Judith.

'Gosh, but coppers are so polite these days,' I smirked.

'New regime,' she said. 'Bit different to your day, Dad.'

'Well let's press on. You never know what we might find.'

She pulled a face in reply.

We started at the top and knocked on a lot of doors which stayed closed. No-one appeared, not even the young mum I'd seen before. But when we got to Campbell's flat the door opposite was ajar and a dark eye twinkled through the gap over a security chain. 'Hello,' said Judith. 'Police.'

'Is it about the break in the other day?' said the voice that belonged to the eye.

'Yes and no,' said Judith. 'It's a follow up about Mr Campbell's death. Have you got a minute?'

The door closed as the chain was released, then opened wide as a small elderly woman came into view. 'I called the police,' she said, 'when I heard someone kick down the door, but they took ages, and then they were just kids. Couldn't catch a cold if you ask me. Some police,' she added for our benefit.

'Yes, we know about the break in,' said Judith, giving me a look again.

'You'd better come in,' said the old lady and stepped back to let us in.

'I'm Detective Sergeant Smith,' said Judith. This is my colleague Detective Constable Granger.'

As I predicted, the old lady didn't ask for our ID. Some people never learn.

We crossed the threshold into a small flat, as warm and neat as a pin.

She sat us down on a sofa and asked, 'Cuppa tea?'

I could see Judith was going to refuse, so I dived in and spoke for the first time 'Love one,' I said, 'milk and two sugars please.'

Judith frowned, but I just gave her a smile, and she opened a notebook she'd pulled from her handbag. 'And you are?' she said to the lady.

'Didn't they tell you?' she said. 'You're the third lot I've seen.'

'Sorry,' I said quickly, remembering the new regime. 'We've only just come aboard. Sickness, Christmas holidays, you know how it is. Short of manpower.'

'Well I pay enough council tax,' she said as she went into the kitchen. 'Should have enough coppers if you ask me. Mayor Ken was always going on about it. New bloke's no different. But you never see any walking about round here. Bloomin' disgrace if you ask me. Yobs on every corner wearing hoodies. I never go out after dark these days.' It was obviously an old sore.

'I know love,' I said sweetly. 'Believe me, we hear it all the time.'

'Dunning,' she said over the sound of the electric kettle heating up.

'Beg pardon,' I said.

'Dunning. Elsie Dunning,' she said, sticking her head round the kitchen door. 'Mrs. Though my Bert's been in the ground for ten years.'

'I'm sorry,' I said sympathetically. This was certainly a morning for apologies.

'No need to be. He wasn't worth a light when he was here. I'm better off without. At least I don't have to listen to him snoring nowadays.'

I really didn't have an answer to that.

27

Elsie delivered the tea in fine china on a tray complete with a plate of biscuits. Very welcome it was too, at least to me.

Judith got stuck in to her questions, ignoring the brew. 'Did you know Mr Campbell well?' she asked.

'Just to say hello to.'

'Did you see anything on the night he died?'

'No. But I heard a bang around ten as I was going to bed.'

'Did you report it?'

'Don't you know? Course I did. It's very quiet here.'

'Did you see anyone around that time. Strangers?' I interjected.

'No. Like I said, I was getting ready for bed.'

'Did he have a lot of visitors?' asked Judith.

'I keep telling you, I've answered all these questions

before. Why are you asking them again?' Elsie might have been old, but she was far from stupid.

'OK Mrs Dunning,' I said. 'We'll come clean.'

'You're not coppers,' she said, looking at each of us in turn, scrutinising us. It was a statement, not a question.

'I used to be,' I said. 'This is my daughter Judith. She still is, but not from your local station.'

'I thought there was something about the pair of you,' said Elsie. 'In the eyes. And aren't you a bit old to still be a constable?' That was for me.

'But I'm on suspension,' Judith said.

'What for?'

'Perverting the course of justice. That's...'

'It was Elsie's turn to interrupt. 'I know what that is,' she said. 'I watch telly. *The Bill*, *Prime Suspect*. Pity real police ain't as smart. The ones who've been round here are a bit thick if you ask me.'

I nodded.

'And maybe taking part in the murder of Thomas Campbell,' Judith went on. 'That's why we're here. I'm trying to clear my name.'

'Did you?' asked Elsie.

'No,' said Judith. 'But someone wants my bosses to think I did.'

'Are you going to hurt me?' asked Elsie.

'God no,' I said. 'Are you going to call the real police?'

'Grass you up?' she said. 'No. I haven't had such excitement since Bert died. More tea?'

'Please,' I said, smiling at Elsie. 'I'm gasping.'

28

When there was more tea and biscuits on the table we got down to business. I could tell Elsie had more information for us, and she didn't disappoint.

'I didn't like those real coppers,' she said, with a sour purse of her lips. 'Too clever by half. Thought I was a bit senile I expect.'

'You're far from that,' I said.

'Now don't try and get round me with flannel,' she said.

I had to smile. 'I wouldn't dream of it Elsie.'

'Wouldn't even have a cup of tea.'

'They didn't know what they were missing,' I said, taking another sip.

'So what *is* your name?' she asked me.

'Nick,' I said. It was good to tell the truth for once.

'You been away? Got a good colour there. That's

another reason I figured you weren't police.'

'A long holiday,' I said. 'In the sun.'

'And you came back for your girl?' She nodded at Judith.

'That's what fathers are for.'

'So how can I help?'

'Tell us what you know about Campbell.'

'A bit. He was queer of course. Gay they call it now don't they? I don't think he *was* very gay though. Not like it used to mean.'

'Why's that?'

'Miserable little sod, pardon my French. But I wouldn't wish him being murdered.'

'But you used to speak?' said Judith.

'Usual stuff. Good morning, nice day, that sort of thing.'

'But not friends?' Me again.

'No.'

'Did he have many friends?' I asked.

'A few. I keep an eye out.'

I bet you do, I thought. 'Anyone in particular?'

'A few. But I tell you what...'

'What?' I asked.

'Place to find out is a pub round the corner. Elkin Arms. The cottage they call it. Don't know why.'

I was sure she did.

'They all go there. There's always been homos round here.' No political correctness for our Elsie, I could tell. 'Ever since the war. Famous ones too. Bloke used to make records over the leather shop. My boy used to buy them. I told him to keep well clear.'

'Joe Meek,' I said.

'You knew him too?'

'Knew of him.'

'Far from meek though he was. He used to get into a right fuss in the market. Shot his landlady. Nice woman. Then himself. Yes. The Elkin Arms is the place to find out about Mr. Campbell's friends.'

'He went there?'

'Bound to have.'

'It's worth a try.' I looked at my watch. Opening time soon. 'Did you tell the real police about it?'

'No. Like I said, they looked down their noses at me.'

'Good,' I said. 'But of course they might put two and two together.'

'And make sixteen most likely,' said Elsie. 'More tea?'

29

This time we refused. 'Thanks for the chat Elsie,' I said as we got ready to leave. 'And the tea.'

'Will you let me know what happens?' she asked.

'Course we will,' I said.

'And good luck to you both. I'll say a prayer for you.'

'Thanks,' said Judith, and gave the old lady a kiss on the cheek.

'Take care,' said Elsie as she shut the door behind us. 'There's bad people out there.'

She didn't know how prescient her words were.

Elsie had given us directions to the pub, which was just off Holloway Road. We walked there and the doors were being unlocked as we arrived. The pub was empty except for the barman, who retreated behind the jump as we walked across the wooden floors. It was just a north

London pub. Nothing special. No gingham flounces or boy band posters on the walls giving clues to the clientele. The barman was a big geezer in T-shirt and jeans with well defined arm muscles, but his voice belonged to a different bloke altogether – high and sibilant with a pronounced lisp. 'Help you?' he asked.

Judith flashed her warrant and said, 'police.'

He didn't look impressed.

'We're here about Thomas Campbell,' she went on.

The barman shrugged. 'Don't know him. Sorry.'

'We heard he used to frequent your establishment,' I said.

'Used?'

'He's dead,' said Judith. 'Murdered. He lived right round the corner.'

'Sorry to hear it, but...' The barman shrugged again. 'Do you want something to drink?'

'Not on duty,' I said.

'Then, I've got to get bottled up,' and he walked away. Just like that. Walked away.

'Fucking hell,' I said to Judith. 'Is that how people treat coppers these days...? Oi, cunt, come here.' I took the tool I'd bought at the hardware store out of my pocket and banged it on the counter. It was a large nail gun. I punched one into the wood of the bar.

The barman stood transfixed at my action, his mouth literally hanging open.

'I said come here,' I said.

And he did, as I punched more nails into the jump.

'We're fuckin' old Bill,' I said. 'And you don't fuckin' walk away from us when we're talking to you. It's not polite.'

'I'm sorry,' he said, looking like he meant it.

'You'll be fuckin' sorrier if you're not careful Doris,' I said. 'You can talk to us here or down the nick. Your choice.'

Bang. Another nail punctured the wood.

I took his silence to mean he wanted to talk at the pub. Just as well, as we didn't have a nick to go to.

'And if you tell me lies I'll have your dick out of your strides and staple it to the bar. Get me?' Though he might enjoy that, of course.

The barman nodded.

'Now. Thomas Campbell. Shot dead in his flat a stone's throw from here just the other day. You know about it don't you?'

The barman nodded again.

'He drank here didn't he?'

He nodded once more.

'I want to know if he had a boyfriend, a partner, a lover, a significant other. Get me?'

Another nod.

'Does that mean he did?'

Nod five.

'So where do I find this mystery man?'

He finally spoke. 'Kebab shop by the station. Tiko's. He works there.'

'Name?'

'Cedric.'

'If you're having me on...'

'No. Cedric. S'true.' He stammered a little and I felt bad about scaring him, but needs must.

'OK. Now give us two large Jack Daniels on ice.'

He did as he was told.

Fuck duty.

30

When we'd finished our drinks, I called the barman over again. 'Just one thing,' I said.

'What?'

'We're going to go look for Cedric now, and I don't want any phone calls being made to warn him off. Get me?'

'I get you.'

'Make sure you do, or we'll be back with the good old public health in tow. And you know what that means.'

'I know,' he still looked terrified.

'Good.' And we left.

'Think that'll work?' said Judith, as we headed towards the station. She'd been silent throughout the whole exchange.

'Always used to.'

'You're in the dark ages Dad. Times have changed.'

'You can say that again. Nobody seems scared of the police anymore.'

'Like I said, times have changed.'

We saw the kebab shop, with its gaudy neon sign lit, as we went down the Holloway Road. 'That's the place,' I said, and as I did so, a little geezer came charging out and headed for the station. 'And that'll be Cedric I reckon. Looks like someone's still frightened of cops,' as I broke into a run.

We almost collided at the entrance. 'Cedric,' I said, as I grabbed him by the arm.

'What? Never heard of him. Let me go.'

'No son,' I said, dragging him towards the corner of the road next to the station. 'I just want a word.'

Judith caught us up as I shoved him against a wall. 'Still fast on your feet,' she said to me.

'When I have to be. Now son, we need some information, and no one will get hurt.'

'I'll call the police,' he said, in a thick accent it was difficult to place.

'We are the police,' said Judith, flashing the fake warrant. 'And you are nicked.'

He seemed to shrink in front of our eyes.

'Unless,' I said.

'Yeah?'

'You tell us what we want to know, and you can get back to the chilli sauce.'

'What do you want?'

'You *are* Cedric then?' said Judith.

He nodded. 'I've done nothing wrong.'

'Then why the runner?'

'My friend's been murdered, and you lot turn up all heavy handed. What do you expect?'

'And no one's been to see you before?'

'He shook his head. 'We didn't live together,' he said. 'I've got my own place. How did you find out about me?'

'A little bird told us,' I said

That didn't appear to register.

'You didn't do it did you?' I asked.

'Christ no. We were together. An item. I loved him.'

'That's never stopped people killing each other before,' I said.

'No, honestly. You must believe me.' I thought he was going to cry.

'I believe you son,' I said. 'Like I said, we just want some information.'

'What information?'

'His computer password,' said Judith. 'He did have a computer didn't he?'

'Is that all? Why didn't you say?' spluttered Cedric.

'We just did,' I said.

'And you'll leave me alone?' His eyes still looked fearful.

'Never met you,' I said.

'Minogue,' he said.

'Minogue,' I echoed. 'Like Kylie?'

'That's it. He was a big fan. Loved her.'

'Why didn't we think of that?' said Judith.

'I hope you're telling us the truth,' I said.

'Course I am. I just want to be left alone.'

'OK, then,' I said, letting him go, and smoothing out his jacket. 'Have a nice day.'

He ducked under my arm and vanished round the corner.

'Did you believe him?' said Judith.

'There were Kylie Minogue CD's everywhere in the flat,' I said. 'But then there were Dusty Springfield and Liza Minelli albums too. And loads more. It makes sense. And he was terrified.'

'Well, let's go and see,' she said.

'Fine. But what about that bloody barman? I told him not to phone.'

'Leave him,' she said. 'Let's not push our luck.'

31

We went to Judith's flat, which was just as she'd described it to me, a garden flat with an entrance in the basement. I'd never thought that sort of arrangement was safe for a woman living alone even a copper who was trained to fight. But she was an adult and it was her choice. She booted up the computer and stuck in the memory stick. When the request for a password came up, she typed MINOGUE in capitals. 'Fingers crossed,' she said, as the screen burst into a rainbow, cleared and a bunch of file icons appeared.

'Result,' she said.

'Good old Cedric,' I said.

She clicked the pointer on one of the icons, and the screen changed again, revealing a dozen or so miniature photographs.

'Is that what I think it is?' I said, looking over her shoulder.

Another click and the first photo filled the screen. It was *exactly* what I thought it was. Two naked men engaged in sexual activity in an anonymous hotel bedroom. One of them was looking straight at the camera, the other face down on the bed being penetrated from behind. 'I know him,' said Judith.

'What personally?'

'No. He's a premiership footballer. Blimey, he's always seen about town with some page three dollybird on his arm.'

'Seems like he changed his style,' I said.

'Go and make us a drink Dad,' she said, 'while I look at the rest. You're making me nervous, hovering over me.'

'What you got?' I asked.

'Gin, whiskey, JD, white rum in the cupboard. Beer, wine and mixers in the fridge.'

'Yes, you *are* a Sharman,' I said, and went to see what I could find in the open plan kitchen.

I made two Malibu and orange juices with ice and a slice. Figured they'd remind me of the island.

When I got back, Judith was staring at the screen, the notebook in front of her filled with names.

'What's cooking?' I asked.

'This is bloody amazing. There's loads of celebs having it off. Mostly with people they shouldn't.' She took her drink and downed a long swig. 'These pictures are worth a fortune to a blackmailer.'

'Mr Campbell?'

'Well I knew he was a slippery customer. Always had his nose in someone else's business. That's what made him such a good snout. But this... '

'Seem them, all?' I asked.

'Not yet. You sit down and make yourself comfortable.'

So I did. We both lit up cigarettes and Judith kept going through the photos. 'Some of these are really sick,' she said.

'All gay?' I asked.

'Far from it. All sorts.'

'No children I hope,' I said, suddenly feeling queasy.

'No, thank Christ. Looks like they're all above the age of consent, but some of them are barely over the line, I reckon.'

Then after a few minutes silence, she said, 'oh my God. I don't believe it.'

'What?' I asked.

'Come see.'

I got up and went over to her desk. On the screen was a youngish bloke, shagging a dark haired woman on another bed. His head was flung back in full *coitus* it seemed and he was thrust deep between her legs. 'What?' I asked.

'Guess who?'

'No idea.'

'He's Job.'

'On the job, more like.'

'And some. He's the bloody assistant commissioner,' she exclaimed.

'My my,' I said. 'He only looks about twelve.'

'You are getting old Dad,' she said with grin. 'Policeman looking younger and all that.'

'Very amusing. At least it's a woman he's doing the business with.'

'But the wrong woman. He's married with a young kid and another on the way. And this sure ain't his wife. I've seen her at a do.'

'Naughty, naughty,' I said. 'I wonder if he knows this photo exists.'

'If he did,' she said, 'it's a good motive for getting rid of Campbell.'

'Don't jump to conclusions,' I replied. 'Seems like a lot of people might have a motive.' I pointed to the screen, filled with the thumbnails of celebrities in compromising positions.

'But he's the only one who could put me in the frame so easily.'

'Good point,' I said.

32

'Well, before we get into all that, is there any chance of anything to eat? I'm starving,' I asked, rubbing my rumbling stomach.

'I'm good on booze, but not on food,' she replied.

'Another Sharman trait,' I said.

'I remember. But there's a good Chinese round the corner.' She looked at her watch. 'And plenty of time for a late lunch. They never chase you out.'

'A Chinky,' I said. 'Been a long time since I had a British Chinese.'

'We don't say Chinky any more Dad,' she scolded. 'I guess you only eat Caribbean, then?' she said.

'Fusion, the bloke who cooks at the bar calls it. I eat his food more than I eat my own.'

'I'd like to visit sometime,' she said.

'You're always welcome. You know that.'

'I'll remember.'

'But I warn you, it's a bit primitive.'

'Dad, where you lived in London was *always* a bit primitive.'

'Thanks,' I said.

We left the flat. The restaurant was less than ten minutes walk away, and still buzzing with the lunch crowd.

We got a table upstairs on the mezzanine by the window and I ordered a bottle of white wine whilst we chose our food. As it had been a while Judith let me order all my old favourites. Crab meat and sweetcorn soup to start. Crispy chilli beef, sweet and sour pork, special fried rice, fried noodles, and mixed veg to follow. Just the job.

It was great to sit down with Judith, even under the circumstances. 'Funny,' I said, after the waiter had poured two glasses of wine. 'We haven't had a chance to talk properly since I got back.'

'Well it's not exactly been old home week has it?' she replied.

'No. You're right there. Even so, it's been a long time since we had a sit down with a decent meal.'

There was always the Ikea meatballs.'

'Yeah. But somehow it didn't have the ambience of this place.'

'You always did love a Chinese lunch. I can remember you taking me for some real feasts in the old days.'

'Good times.'

'Yeah.'

'So, no bloke in your life?'

'Don't beat around the bush Dad will you?'

'It's a simple enough question love.'

'With a simple answer. No.'

'But there must've been some.'

'I'm a big girl Dad, I have had a few blokes in my life in the last seven years. There *was* one,' she said almost wistfully.

'Job?'

'Course,' she replied. 'Inevitable. You know how it goes.'

'Not married I hope?'

'No, worse – divorced with two young kids. So when his ex called, he dropped everything and went to sort her problems out.'

'Dropped everything – including you.'

'Got it in one. It was as if she knew when we had something planned and one of the kids would get sick or the boiler would break down and off he'd go like a poodle. Can't blame him really, but it just started to get on my nerves. Christ, if we'd moved in together or got married...' She trailed off. 'It doesn't bear thinking about. There were rows, he'd get guilty. Only thing, I never knew who made him more guilty. Me, or her.'

'So just the one in all this time?'

'Dad. You don't know how difficult it is for a female cop these days to have a relationship. I mean, I dated one bloke. Went back to his flat and he only had soya milk in the fridge. And no sugar. And no booze.'

'Tragic.'

'You can say that again. And he was a member of CO 19. A real gung ho sharpshooter.'

The soup arrived in steaming bowls and we dived in. Bloody good it was too. When the dishes had been cleared away and the main course served, juggling some mange tout with my chopsticks, I said, trying to be nonchalant, 'I was thinking about your mum last night.'

'Me too.' replied Judith. 'Time of the year I suppose.'

'With me it's the time of life too.' I looked down at the table. 'Delicate subject,' I said.

'Not really. Not any more. It's history isn't it Dad?'

'You know what they say about history. Those that don't learn from it are condemned to making the same mistakes over and over again. Or something like that.'

'Still making mistakes Dad?'

'Not as many as I did.'

'That still leaves you a lot of leeway.' Judith said pointedly.

The mange tout dropped back into my bowl. 'Should have got a spoon and fork,' I said.

'Don't change the subject.'

'Sorry.' I took a sip of my wine. 'So where were you planning on spending Christmas. Not like you are I'm sure.'

'You're changing the subject again,' said Judith, but with a smile. 'Funnily enough with some friends of Mum's and Louis's.'

Louis had been the man who my wife married after she divorced me. They both died in a plane crash in America years ago with their new son. Luckily Judith hadn't been with them.

'They lived in the next village,' she went on. 'They have a daughter my age. Married of course with kids. We're still friends.'

Louis had taken early retirement from his dental practice and bought a house in Kent. A converted oast house.

'She was happy there with Louis and David and me,' said Judith wistfully.

David had been the son.

I suddenly realised how lonely my daughter was and it almost broke my heart.

'An oast house,' I said, trying to break the mood. 'That takes me back. We went to Hastings once for the day on the train before you were born. God knows why. Passed loads. She always said she'd love to live in one.'

'And she did. For a few years. Living the quiet life. Making cakes for the village fete.'

'She never made cakes for me.'

'Always you Dad, eh?' Judith was shaking her head.

'Come on. I didn't mean anything. It's just not how I saw her ending up. The WI or whatever. Living the idyllic countryside dream.'

'She enjoyed it. I think your old life changed her perspective. Sometimes the noisy life gets too noisy Look at us now.'

I reflected on that for a moment, thought about my Caribbean island and knew she was telling the truth.

'You know I never meant to hurt her. Or you.' I wondered if I looked as ashamed as I felt.

'I know. It was just hard to deal with, that's all.'

'I was young then. Stupid. I know that now. Where I've been there's a lot of time to think. Think about the past. The mistakes I made. The people I hurt.'

'Oh Dad. Don't get maudlin.'

'I won't. But I mean it. I treated her so badly. Sometimes like a piece of shit on my shoe. If you think I'm not ashamed you've got me wrong.'

'But the other women? The drinking. The drugs?'

'It was the times. Everyone did it. Especially in the CID as it was then. Lads culture. You must've seen it.'

'Of course. Especially with my surname.'

'I'm sorry for that too – like I keep saying. But then you could've used Louis' name.'

'I'm a Sharman for good or evil. It would all have come out sooner or later anyway. It always does.'

'Yeah, I suppose. But I'm proud you used my name. Prouder than you'll ever know.'

She touched my hand. 'I'm glad,' she said.

'And I wish I'd not done what I did. Especially the other women. It was like a competition.'

'I don't think I want to hear any more.'

She was right. She didn't need any details. But it *had* been like a competition in the force in the eighties. Which of us could shag the most women, drink the most, snort the most cocaine. Even if you didn't want to join in, you more or less had to, or take the flak. The last thing you wanted to be was an outsider. Otherwise one day the person you wanted watching your back just might not be there.

'Fair enough,' I said. 'I just wish I'd had time to tell her how sorry I was.'

'Perhaps in the next life,' said Judith.

'Perhaps,' I replied. 'But let's not go there.'

33

'So tell me about your island,' she said when the plates were empty and more wine was on its way.

'Great place,' I replied, looking out of the window at the freezing streets full of miserable looking people heading for the tube. 'Not like here. Warm weather helps. And people know how to enjoy themselves without spending much money. Not racing to keep up with the neighbours.'

'I *will* come and visit you know.'

'You should've done years ago. Lots of eligible young men.'

'And eligible older ones, like you?' she teased.

'Could be.' I pictured Rita in my mind's eye. 'There was one woman. But it went nowhere. Now that I think about it, I may try and revive the flame when I get back.'

'I hope it works for you. Wedding on the beach?'

'Then you'd definitely have to come over. Walk me down the aisle in your best frock.'

Judith laughed. 'So what do you do there?'

'Not much. Kick back. There's a bar a few minutes walk from where I live. Two young guys, Clive and Cyril, run the place. Got an old Wurlie.'

'A what?' she asked.

'Wurlie. Wurlitzer jukebox full of vinyl. Reggae, old rock and roll. Some Blue Note jazz singles I ordered from the mainland. Reminded me of Emerald. Remember him?'

'The black guy that ran a dodgy bar in Clapham?'

'The very same. He used to let you wear that ring of his.'

'Emerald stone. I remember playing with it when I was little.'

'Yeah. It was the size of a house. Great guy. Died couple of years ago now.'

'I'm sorry to hear that.'

'Yeah. Too many people have died. Anyhow, he used to play *Flamingo* by Earl Bostic down in that bar – I got a copy in memory. Sometimes late, me, Clive and Cyril, and some tourist birds they've pulled, we sit up all night watching the tide flow, and play that jukebox and get drunk.'

'No tourists for you?'

'No. They're too young, or else too old and desperate. I want the quiet life.'

'That's not what you're getting here,' she looked concerned.

'We'll sort it out, then I'll go back. I'm getting too old for this lark. This is Sharman's last case. At least, I hope it is.'

I *was* getting maudlin, and thankfully she changed the subject. 'So what do we do about these photographs?'

'Tricky. Your snout obviously had an alternative source of income.'

'Blackmail?'

'Well from what we've seen I doubt he was keeping them for personal use. Not the male on female action, anyway.'

'Do you think Cedric was in on it?'

'Doubtful,' I said. 'I think Mr Campbell had a lot of secrets. There was money, the gun and the computer thingy stashed away at the flat, but Cedric didn't try and get to them. Cedric said he didn't live with him, but he must've had a key, or even if he didn't, it wasn't exactly hard to bust into the place. He would have taken the opportunity to retrieve the pics if he was in on it. No, I don't think he knew about the hiding place, or the photos for that matter. He gave up the password without a murmur, remember.'

'We could always go and see him again. We know where he works.'

'And that's another thing,' I said. 'A poxy kebab shop. Those photos could be worth a fortune in the right hands but Cedric's probably slaving away for the minimum wage. Anyway, I've got a feeling we put the fear of God into him this morning, poor little bugger. I reckon he's flown the coop by now.'

'I'm not surprised he was frightened. You threatening that barman with a bloody nail gun. A bit Jack Regan wasn't it?'

'Jack Regan. You remember him?'

'You gave me the videos remember? Not really suitable viewing for an eleven-year-old, but never mind.'

'Course. Bloody good copper. Then he turned into Inspector Morse. Saddest thing I've ever seen.'

'So what do we do Dad?'

'Find out who set you up for the murder of Campbell. Prime bloody suspect you. Bet you're not the most popular girl in school are you?'

'You got that right.'

'Down to me again I'm afraid,' I said.

'You can't blame yourself for everything.'

'I didn't think I'd ever hear you say that.'

'Well, now you have. Let's draw a line under it Dad.'

'Glad to hear it. The most important thing is that we clear your name, then we'll all get back to normal. One day we'll chat about all this over a rum punch at the beach. Right now, we should get in touch with the Assistant Commissioner – see what he's got to say for himself.'

'Bloody hell,' she said.

34

'That'll be fun,' said Judith.

'Got to be done.' I insisted. I knew she would be worried, naturally, but confronting the commissioner was our only option.

'Of course. It's just...'

'Just what?' I asked. 'End of your career? You know we're going to sort this. Have faith.'

'Of course I have faith. You're here. Frankly, I'm not much worried about my career just now.'

'Whatever happens, we've got to get rid of this stupid murder charge,' I reminded her.

'Easier said than done. And that's it. One person has been killed already – it must be about those photos. I don't want us to be next on the list.'

'We won't. Not while we have them anyway.'

'Campbell had them, remember. And it didn't stop whoever did it.'

'Good point,' I said. 'But let's not look on the down side. Are you ready to make a call to Scotland Yard? Dig out the AC, and let him know that we know he's been a very bad boy.'

'Ready as I'll ever be, I suppose.'

'Then grasp the nettle love. The sooner the better.'

'So what's the plan?'

'You remember Occam's Razor?' I said.

'Of course. I did go to university you know.'

'So did I, for a bit. Until they politely asked me to leave. Not so politely actually.'

'I know that Dad. I *finished* my course and got a degree – remember?'

'All right clever clogs. And I didn't mean to patronise you. Right, old William of Occam reckoned that the simplest explanation was often the correct one. Right?'

'Right.'

'So let's go with Occam's plan. The simpler the better. Just tell the AC that you have information about Campbell's murder, and you want to meet him. What's his name by the way?'

'Turner. Malcolm Turner, OBE, to be exact.'

'Nice. Tell him you'll meet him somewhere out of the office. You turn up. So do I. I have the pictures. We confront him, and we ask... No. demand his help. Otherwise the piccies go to *his* boss. Or the newspapers.'

'Blackmail?'

'Pure and simple. You got a problem with that?'

'Not if it works. But maybe Campbell tried that – and look where he ended up.'

'We'll be better prepared than your squealer but I think you'd better make yourself scarce from your flat for a while. Just in case.'

'I've nowhere to go.'

'I think my mate Pierre can find you a crib at my hotel. He's very fond of fifty pound notes, is our Pierre.'

'Lucky you've got the money.'

'Ain't it just.' I winked.

'So when do we make the call?'

'Sooner the better. Let's finish up here, and do the deed.'

'OK, Dad. Want some pudding first? They've got banana fritters. They always were your favourite.'

35

After lunch we went back to Judith's flat to pick up her bits and pieces. While she packed a bag, I phoned the hotel and good old Pierre was most accommodating. I explained I needed another bed. His tone told me that he thought I'd pulled a mystery, but I didn't bother to put him right. He informed me that a suite had become available after a late cancellation, and it was mine – for a mindboggling amount per night. The credit crunch obviously hadn't reached the world of luxury hotels yet. Two bedrooms, two baths, sitting room, the works. I told him I'd take it for the foreseeable. He told me he'd have my stuff transferred again. I thanked him, said I'd see him all right. He replied that he knew that I would. I bet he didn't even blush.

That done, Judith made the call. It took her an age to

get put through to the AC. But eventually she spoke his name, and told him that she had some intel about Campbell's death that she needed to pass on. From what I could gather from the one-sided conversation, he didn't seem keen on a meet, but eventually gave in. and she told him the name of a boozer on the embankment I'd suggested, and a time she'd be there. Five-thirty that evening.

We shot back to the hotel in a cab, and Pierre himself showed us to the suite. Nice place. Penthouse style with a great view of Hyde Park, and a complimentary bowl of fruit, flowers and champagne. I explained that Judith was my daughter, but I don't think he believed me. I didn't care. He accepted a nifty fifty, then stood with his hand out again for another. Once again he didn't even miss a beat.

My stuff was all lined up in one of the bedrooms, and Judith stashed hers in the other and took a bath. Might as well use the facilities I thought. I sat down and watched a re-run of *Midsomer Murders* on the big screen TV. Might as well get back into the mood I thought.

At quarter to five I took the laptop in its bag and got it stored in the safe in my bedroom. I wasn't about to turn up with all the evidence. Just the photos we'd printed off. I left alone and took a cab to the pub, arrived at just after five, got an *Evening Standard* from a vendor, went inside, ordered a pint and sat at the window watching the river traffic go by.

Judith arrived twenty minutes later, ignored me,

bought a gin and tonic and sat a few tables away from mine.

Game on.

At five-thirty on the dot, a dark-haired man I recognised from the photos came in alone, wearing civvies. He quickly saw Judith and headed in her direction. They shook hands in a perfunctory way and he sat. There was a short conversation, and I then thought it was time to join the party, leaving my drink and heading towards them. He looked up as I loomed over the table. 'Hello Malcolm,' I said. 'Want to see some pretty pictures?'

36

The photos were in an eight-by-ten brown envelope that I dropped on the table between Turner and Judith. He looked up at me in surprise, then recognition dawned in his eyes as they moved from me to my daughter and back. 'It can't be,' he said. 'Nick Sharman. You're supposed to be dead.'

'Sorry to spoil a good story. I didn't think you'd know me, being of a different generation.'

'My God. Everyone knows you. You're a bloody legend. The man who gets away with everything and disappears into thin air.'

I shrugged.

'So where have you been? I see by your tan it wasn't local.'

'That's between me and my travel agent,' I said.

'Aren't you wanted for something?' he asked. 'What's to stop me taking out my phone and getting you nicked?'

'Perhaps you should look in that envelope first,' I said.

He pulled out the sheaf of copies of the photographs. His face went stark white as he looked at them.

'Christ,' he said. 'Where the hell did you get these?'

'You look like you need a drink,' I said. 'What'll you have?'

'A scotch,' he replied. 'A large one.'

I went to the bar, ordered his drink, collected mine on the way back and took a seat at the table. He gulped down a mouthful of whisky and coughed harshly.

'Still going to have me nicked?' I asked.

He shook his head slowly. 'What do you want?' he asked.

'A number of things,' I replied. 'But it's not me that wants them. It's my daughter.' Judith was silent but I could see the steely determination in her eyes, so like my own.

'Christ,' he said again, a little colour having returned to his skin. 'What a pair you are.'

'She's up on a murder charge,' I said. 'It needs to go away.'

'Just like that? It's not down to me.'

'Come on,' I said. 'The whole thing is a farce.'

'How do you know? You weren't there.'

'Nor was she,' I said. 'I know my daughter. And the fact that you're so quick to deny it means you know there's more to it. Anyway, he was her snout, and a damn good one by all accounts. Why kill the goose that lays the golden egg?' I echoed my earlier words to Judith.

'They'd fallen out, according to her DS,' said Turner, looking at Judith. 'He wasn't coming up with the goods anymore. Right?'

The question was addressed to her, and she spoke for the first time. 'He was getting sloppy,' she replied. 'Leading me on wild goose chases.'

'So the goose was going off piste instead of laying,' said Turner. 'And there was money missing.'

'She doesn't need money,' I said.

'Due to the fruits of your last little labour I imagine,' he said, sneering. 'I remember now. That bank job in the city that destroyed a whole building and killed the perpetrators in the blaze. I always heard it was down to you.'

'That's history,' I said. 'Nothing proven.'

'Times change, and so does forensic science. You'd be amazed at what might have turned up in what? Seven, eight years?'

'Don't threaten me pal,' I said, moving closer to him, and tapping my finger on the papers in front of him. 'I hear you're "happily married",' the implication being clear in my voice, 'and want to continue climbing the slippery pole of promotion. We have the originals of these, and by God we'll use them to bring you down unless you pull your finger out.'

'OK,' he said, looking as sick as a dog. 'But it won't be easy – and what's to stop you using them anyway?'

'Trust us, son,' I said. 'It's the only thing you *can* do.'

"Where are the originals?" he asked.

37

'So where are the originals of these?' asked Turner.

'Somewhere safe and sound,' I replied.

'Where did you get them?'

'Campbell's flat,' I said.

'How the hell did he get them?'

'I doubt we'll ever know,' I said. 'Have you been approached before?'

He shook his head.

'So who's the girl?' I asked.

'I'd rather not say,' he said, flushing

'You'll say what we want to hear,' I said.

'Just someone I met. Look, I really...'

'Spit it out Malcolm,' I interrupted. 'Don't be shy.'

'At a conference.'

'I see. A tart,' I said. 'Where?'

'What does it matter?'

'It might matter to your wife and children.'

'OK,' he said, looking shamefaced now. 'It was at a hotel in the West End. An international conference of top brass officers. I was staying over. It was easier. There was a lot of drinking in the evening after dinner. You know what happens at those sort of things.'

'I was never a top copper,' I said. 'But I can imagine.'

'She was in the bar,' he went on. 'We connected. We went to my room.'

'Which was all set up with a camera.'

'I didn't know that.'

'But someone knew you'd be there, and she was sent after you.'

'Obviously. I was a bloody fool.'

'And you have had no approaches by anyone for money or a favour?' I couldn't work it out. Why would someone go to so much trouble to set him up and then not act on it?

'Not until now.'

'Well it wasn't us who arranged it son. When was this?'

'Three months ago. Early autumn.'

'Someone's patient,' said Judith. She was obviously thinking on the same lines as I was.

'Are there others?' he asked.

'Others?' I questioned.

'Other photographs. Other people.'

'Oh yeah,' I said. 'Lots. Now. I think it's time for you to go and have a think about what you're going to do for

Judith. And remember, we're not in the game of breaking up families. You play ball, and you can have the originals of these.'

' I understand,' he said. 'But are they the originals? Did Campbell have more? Or someone else? Are what you have just copies?' It all came out in a rush.

I suddenly felt sorry for the bloke. It could have so easily been me twenty years ago, sitting there with evidence of my wrongdoing on the table. 'No idea,' I said. 'Who was originally behind this is a mystery. Campbell himself, accomplices – don't ask us. Just watch your back. But believe me, Judith is my main concern. And when this is all over, I don't want to hear that she's being treated as a scapegoat. I want her fully exonerated and her career restored. If that's what she wants.'

The look he gave me told me that would never happen. But first things first.

38

Turner got up from the table and said. 'I'll be going then.'

I nodded.

He went to leave but I stopped him. 'I think you've forgotten something.'

'What?'

I tapped the envelope again. 'Something to remind you of what you're going to do.'

'I suppose,' he said gloomily, picking up the envelope like it contained a live scorpion and exiting the pub.

After he'd left, Judith said, 'I hated that.'

'I could tell,' I said. 'You hardly said a word.'

'You made up for it.'

'Had to be done.' I wasn't ashamed of what I'd said to Turner. I'd have done worse to clear my daughter's name.

'I don't like blackmail.'

'I don't like you being up on charges.'

'Do you think he was telling the truth?' she asked. 'About not being approached?'

'He looked pretty shocked when he saw the photos. Could be he was surprised there were more than one lot. Could be he had no idea they existed at all. Who knows? Who cares, as long as he does what he's told.'

'It won't be that easy. Not even for an AC.'

'Sweetheart,' I said. 'He wants to be Commissioner, I could tell. He had ambition coming out of his ears. Did you see him flinch when I mentioned talking to his superiors? He'll do something, even if it's only to get some other poor bugger stitched up for the crimes. My bet is you'll be reinstated within a week. Just in time for new year, if not before.'

'I hope you're right Dad. Although I don't know if I want to go back on the strength. I'm feeling a bit disillusioned at the moment.'

'That's your choice love. All I want is for all this to go away, and I can get back to my life, and you to yours – whatever your choice of career.'

'I'll miss you.'

'I'll miss you too. But London's not for me anymore. Too big, too cold, too many people and bad memories.'

'Well, maybe I'll come back with you this time.'

'I mean it about you being very welcome.'

She smiled.

I smiled back at my daughter, we finished our drinks and left.

39

We hailed a cab and headed back to the hotel. 'A drink, then dinner?' I said.

'Sounds like a plan,' said Judith. 'But I need some things, a change of clothes and some underwear. Drop me off at Selfridges,' she said. 'I'll walk back.'

I told the cabbie, who took us into Oxford Street where Judith dived out, then through the back doubles into Park Lane and the hotel – and the drink I'd promised myself.

But as soon as I opened the door to the suite's sitting room, I knew someone else was in there. I could sense it in the changed atmosphere. The lamp I'd left on was still lit, the curtains still drawn, the doors to the bedrooms still shut. Nothing seemed out of place, but I just knew something was deeply wrong.

'Come in, Mr Stark,' said a well modulated voice. 'Or is it Mr Sharman? Don't be shy.'

I stood in the doorway as a figure got up from the armchair facing away from me, towards the dead TV set on the wall. No one I knew, and no one I wanted to know, I was sure of that.

'Do close the door,' he said. 'Don't want anyone getting the wrong idea.'

I did as I was told. The Glock 9 he held loosely in his hand convinced me that he hadn't come to explain how to work the DVD player. He gestured for me to come further inside. Again, I did as I was told. He was in late middle age, bulky inside a decent suit, with grey hair in a crew cut. Ex-military by his bearing, and bloody dangerous I imagined.

'Have a seat,' he said. 'Make yourself comfortable. And where's your daughter? I was so looking forward to meeting her.' There was a faint highland lilt to his voice.

'Late night shopping,' I said. 'You know what women are like. Especially at this time of the year.'

'No problem. We have plenty of time. And don't worry Mr Sharman. No one's going to get hurt. Unless of course you do something stupid.'

'You're the one with the gun.'

'Precisely. Now, I believe you have something I want.'

'Such as?'

'Don't try to play me, Sharman,' he said. 'You know what I mean.'

'I must say he was quick,' I said. 'But how did he know where we were?'

'About whom are we speaking,' he said, smoothly.

'As if you don't know. The Assistant Commissioner of the Metropolitan Police. Malcolm Turner.'

'Sorry,' he said. 'You've got me beat there. I'm afraid we don't share with the locals.'

It took me a moment to get the picture. 'So he didn't send you. And you're not Job.'

'Heaven forbid,' he said. 'All that walking the streets never appealed to me. Now let's get down to business before I make life very difficult for you. And your daughter.'

'Already is for her,' I said. 'So who exactly are you?'

'Let's just say I work for the government,' he replied.

'I gathered that. Five, Six, or are there more numbers these days, in this world of increased security?'

'It really doesn't matter does it, Mr Sharman? But believe me I have the power to see you disappear like a puff of smoke. Especially as you're already travelling on false papers.'

'Identification?' I asked. 'Just for the record.'

He almost laughed, but not quite. 'Take my word for it.'

I had no choice.

'So,' I said. 'How did you catch on?'

'When you broke into Campbell's flat and found what he was hiding, and went looking for the late Mr Campbell's password.'

'You knew about his little sideline?'

'Not his alone I can assure you. And not so little. We

knew he had photographs. But we didn't know where. There was nothing on his home computer.'

'So you broke the password.'

'Not us. The Met's IT boys are hot stuff.'

'But their search teams aren't so hot.'

'Yes. I've had to have a word with them.'

'I thought you didn't share with the locals.'

'We don't. But they share with us. In these times of "increased security" as you so rightly put it yourself.'

'And they don't know you've found us?'

He nodded. 'Need to know basis only,' he said. "And they don't. Not at the moment.'

'So how did you?' I asked. 'Find us, I mean.'

'Oh do come on Sharman. You can't go round antagonising half the gay population of north London without someone letting on. It's not like the old days you know. And impersonating police officers. And doing criminal damage to the public house owned by a large chain who pay a lot in taxes. Haven't you heard of CCTV? You and your daughter weren't exactly discreet. And there's facial recognition software that recognised you both. Then we just went through recent arrivals at ports and airports and there you were. Even with that beard and a few years under your belt it only took a moment. I think you're out of time Mr Sharman.'

He wasn't the first to point that out. I couldn't disagree, no matter if I'd wanted to.

Then, without warning, the door to my bedroom opened and another man emerged. Big bloke, dark suit.

Another hard ex-military bastard – and this one twenty years younger than me. He was holding my Colt .45 in his hand. The pistol I'd taken from Campbell's flat was stuck in his belt, and the bag containing my computer was on his shoulder.

'Bang to rights,' I said.

'Too right,' said my posh friend, who I took to be the boss. 'Now, may we continue? Looks like you struck gold,' he said to his subordinate.

'Two weapons and a laptop complete with memory stick.'

'And that safe was supposed to be thief proof,' I said.

'Piece of piss.'

'Mandatory five years for the weapons,' said the man with the Glock.

'And you're going to turn me in?'

'Probably not. As long as you behave. You can go back to your island paradise and live a long and full life.'

'You know about that – the island?'

'We know quite a lot, believe me.'

I believed him, but I didn't like it. Any of it.

'Well congratulations,' was all I said.

'So now all we need is your daughter,' said the older man, his accent turning more clipped.

Who at that point opened the door to the suite, a yellow Selfridges bag in her hand.

'Do come in,' he added, smiling widely. 'Join the party.'

40

Judith came inside, dropped her bag, and said. 'Visitors. How nice.'

''Fraid not,' I said. 'Spooks. And not the friendly kind. Looks like we're back where we started. They found our little bargaining tool.'

She looked from one of the men to the other. 'Bugger,' she said. 'Just when I thought things were beginning to go right.'

'Do take a seat, Miss Sharman,' said the man with the Glock.

'Detective-Inspector Sharman,' she corrected him, icily.

'Strictly speaking, not at the moment. But we'll let that pass. Do sit though.'

She did as he said and joined me on the sofa. I gave her shoulders a quick squeeze.

'I think we'd better have a look at what you found before we go,' the posh guy said to his pal. 'Besides this business with Assistant Commissioner Turner fascinates me.'

The muscles of the operation, the one who had my stuff sat at the desk, pulled the computer from its bag, plugged in the power line and fired it up. Then he loaded up the memory stick, entered the password and opened the files. He clicked through them quickly until he found what he was looking for. 'Well, well, they were right.'

The man with the Glock walked over and looked over his shoulder. 'Deary me,' he said. 'What would the Commissioner say?'

Then to us he said, 'you did a good job. Thank you. Now we must go, and we'll be taking this equipment – and of course the guns – with us.'

'And what about my daughter?' I said.

'I'm sorry.'

'So that's it. You leave her hanging in the wind?'

'Unfortunately yes. Casualties of war, I'm afraid.' he smarmed.

'No,' I said. 'We do all the work and you just walk away. I don't think so.' I felt myself getting riled, regardless of the gun he held in his fist.

'You have no choice.'

'I'll go to the newspapers.'

'Without proof? They'd laugh you out of there. And there's the question of you ending up in prison. Or of course you could just disappear.'

'You keep saying that. But unless you're prepared to shoot us both here and now, then I'm on the phone the minute you leave.'

'Once again, Mr Sharman, you have no proof once we leave here.'

'Someone will listen. Someone always does. We know some of the people in those photographs,' said Judith, speaking for the first time, 'And there's always the internet. Don't you read the papers? The *Guardian* would have a field day with this.'

'Not to mention the *Telegraph*,' I added.

The man with the gun looked at the other one, then at me. 'You would read the bloody *Telegraph*,' he said. 'All right. What exactly do you want?'

'Simple,' I replied. 'Just what we asked of Turner. A full exoneration for my daughter, and no comeback.'

'It's a possibility,' he said.

'And a proper investigation into Campbell's murder with no stitch ups.'

'That would be down to the Met.'

'And I just vanish with no comeback to me either,' I said.

'We have no interest in you Mr Sharman. You've served your time.'

'Just one more thing,' I said.

He sighed. 'Yes?'

'Who exactly *is* behind the blackmail?'

He smiled. 'Some Russians,' he said. 'A family. Not nice people. It's best that you don't know any more. We are looking into apprehending them.'

'So was it them who murdered Campbell?' I asked.

'Forget about the Russians and Campbell and Turner. Get back on a plane and all will be well. You have my word.'

His word and half a quid would get you a bar of chocolate, but it was all we had.

'Fair enough,' I said.

And with that they both left, taking my computer, the memory stick and the guns with them.

When they'd gone, I looked at Judith who still looked furious, too angry to speak, the colour high in her cheeks. 'How about that drink then?' I said.

41

'So what do you think?' asked Judith when we each had a full glass.

'I think we're fucked,' I said.

'You don't trust him?'

'Do you?'

'I don't know.'

'Nor me. But trust him or not, he's gone, with all the evidence.'

'So what will you do?'

'Find out who killed Campbell. That's all we can do. If we find that, we can get to the bottom of all this.'

'Jesus Dad. It's a bloody long shot.'

'Well I'm not leaving you in the shit.'

'It might be for the best.'

'And have you end up in jail? You know what they do

to coppers in there.'

'I know,' Judith said, her eyes fixed on the carpet.

'You could come with me,' I said softly.

'No passport, remember.'

'There's ways and means to get out of the country. All this EU business. No frontiers anymore, isn't that the deal?'

'It's not as simple as that.'

'Then what about all these illegal immigrants I'm always reading about in the *Telegraph*. If they can get in, surely we can get out. Money's no object.'

'They know where you are don't they?'

'There's nothing much of mine there. Nothing I can't just walk away from. I live the simple life remember?'

'And be on the run for the rest of our lives?' she looked sceptical.

'Beats Holloway. Don't think for too long. They found us easily enough. It's not exactly low profile here you know.'

'I know.'

We ate dinner in the room that night. Neither of us fancied the restaurant. In fact neither of us fancied eating much, but you do what you have to do.

42

'These Russians,' I said, when we were on coffee and brandy. 'Any chance of finding them? You must have some mates left who'll help you.'

'Getting fewer by the hour I reckon,' she said, gloomily. 'And maybe we should wait. I may be exonerated like that bloke said.'

'The man with no name,' I said. 'And Father Christmas might come early this year.'

'I know it's stupid.' she said. 'I'm just getting so tired of all this.'

'Sorry love,' I said. 'I know what you mean. I feel powerless too – but we've got to do everything we can. Tomorrow, first thing, get on the blower and make enquiries. Use up any favours owed, OK?'

'OK Dad. But I'm going to turn in. I'm shattered.'

'Yeah, you do that love. I'm going to sit up for a bit, watch TV.'

'I'll see you in the morning then.'

'Sure. I bet things look different tomorrow.'

'And Father Christmas might come early this year.' She gave me a wan smile, kissed me on the cheek and headed off.

I poured another large one, switched on the TV, quickly turned it off again, and went to bed.

The next morning, after breakfast, Judith told me she wanted to go back to her flat to collect some things. 'Want me to come?' I asked.

'No, don't bother,' she said. 'I won't be long. I'll get a cab there and back.'

'If you're sure?'

'Couldn't be surer.'

'Well, be careful love. This isn't over yet.'

'I'll be fine.'

I sat and tried to do the crossword, but couldn't concentrate. I tried the TV again, but it was filled with mental cases, alcoholics and junkies screaming at each other in barely discernible English, so I kicked that into touch. The radio was no better. Phone-ins by more lunatics, or else music that meant less than nothing to me. So in the end I just sat on the sofa trying to figure out what to do next. I'd been a lousy father. A lousy husband. A lousy copper too. But funnily enough I'd been quite a good private detective. Working on my own suited me. Perhaps I should just grab my daughter and get lost. It was a big world, and we could afford it.

43

Around lunchtime, my mobile rang. Naturally I expected it to be Judith, her being the only one with the number, but instead the voice in my ear belonged to a man with a guttural accent. 'You had something of mine I think, but carelessly lost it. Now I have something of yours. Your daughter.'

I'm not often stuck for words, but I couldn't think of anything to say for a moment. My worst fears had come true. The one person in the world I would die for was in deep trouble, and I was left standing like a fool.

'You don't answer me,' said the voice. 'Perhaps you don't believe me.'

'I believe you,' I said. The spook with the Glock had told us about Russian involvement and if this geezer wasn't Russian, I was a monkey's uncle.

'That is good. Now we talk business.'

'Let me speak to her,' I said. 'And if you've hurt one hair on her head...'

'Shut up. You don't make the terms.'

'Let me speak to her,' I said again.

There was a pause, then Judith came on and said. 'Sorry Dad. I should've listened to you.'

'Are you OK?' I asked.

'I've had better days, but I'll survive.'

'Has he hurt you?'

'They. A pair of right goons. Tell them to fuck off. I have.'

There was a racket at the end of the phone, and the bloke came back on. 'Please tell us to fuck off,' he said. 'And you never find out where your daughter is buried.'

That was the wrong thing to say to me, but I bit my tongue. 'OK,' I said. 'What do you want?'

'We want what belongs to us. It is worth a lot of money.'

'It's gone,' I said. 'If I had it you could have it back, but it was taken from us. That's the truth, I swear.'

'So your daughter said. But do I believe you?'

'Do you think I care about some photos?' I said. 'Listen. She means more to me than anything.'

'I believe you. She is a beauty. It would be a shame to ruin that.' I felt the familiar red mist, but struggled to keep my anger in check.

'Don't even think about it.'

'Then I need money.'

'How much?'

He named a figure.

'I can do that,' I said.

'Then you can do twice as much.'

'And you keep doubling the figure.'

'Until the pips squeak, as I believe is one of your English sayings.'

'The pips are squeaking, believe me.'

'Then get the money. Tomorrow.'

'Come on,' I said. 'I can't just go to a hole in the wall. That's a lot of cash. It's not even in this country. It will need organising.'

'How soon then?'

'Two days at least. Maybe three.'

'You have until the day before Christmas Eve.'

Three days.

'I'll get it.'

'You'd better. Our hospitality to your daughter runs out then. We'll be in touch.' He gave me a mobile phone number, then hung up.

You've just signed your own death warrant, I thought. You don't know it yet, but you're a dead man walking. You, your family, and anyone else involved.

44

I looked at my watch. Too early to do anything about the money yet, but I couldn't sit still, keyed-up with tension and fear about Judith's whereabouts. I reckoned a trip to Judith's place would keep me occupied, and stop me from going out of my mind. I might discover something that would lead me to the Russians, her kidnappers.

I dressed casually, tooled up with all that I had left – my nail gun and jemmy – left the hotel, grabbed a lobster on Park Lane and headed for Camden. The cabbie wanted to chat, but one look at my boat in the mirror shut him up.

When he dropped me off I went down the steps to the flat door that was almost invisible from the street. It was ajar. I'd been right about the arrangement not being a good one. As I didn't have a key that was the reason for the jemmy, but I didn't need it.

I hate open doors. I've found some dreadful things on the other side of them in my life. But at least I knew Judith was alive. Not like the last time I'd gone through one, and found my lover dead on the other side.

The door wasn't damaged as far as I could see, and I pushed it open slowly, the nail gun in one fist, the jemmy in the other. Neither would be much good against armed men, but they made me feel better. The inside of the flat had that dead feeling that empty dwellings do.

There was a short hall with a bathroom on one side and a bedroom the other. At the end was a large living room with an open-plan kitchen on one side where I'd prepared our drink what seemed like just hours earlier, but now felt like a lifetime ago. The far wall was all glass, with patio doors overlooking a scrubby garden. But then it was December, and in the summer it might've been a glorious palette of colour. The place had been turned over, not neatly. But there were no obvious signs of a struggle, and no blood. I was grateful for that. Knowing they'd hurt my girl would have torn me to pieces. Suddenly, I heard a phone ring. The land line telephone was on the floor, the wire pulled out of the wall socket, so I did a three sixty and found Judith's mobile on on the kitchen floor, the small screen showed DCI QUINN was calling. I didn't know any DCI Quinn, and I didn't want him knowing me, so I rejected the call. The battery indicator was low, but luckily there was a charger plugged into one of the wall sockets. I grabbed it, stuck it and the phone into my pocket and left, closing the door.

45

I cabbed it back to the West End and called into a boozer
at the back of the hotel for a pint. I checked Judith's
phone, and the missed calls were starting to pile up from
all sorts. No one I knew obviously. I switched the phone
off to save the battery.

I called my banker that afternoon, when it would be
morning over there. I phoned from a call box off Oxford
Street. It was freezing cold inside, stunk of piss, the
handset felt like it had been dipped in chip fat and it was
decorated with cards for prostitutes of every size, shape,
colour and creed – and every variation of gender that even
a gynaecologist might have trouble recognising. I
wondered how many of the photographs were genuine.

'I'm in London and I need cash,' I said when he
answered promptly. That's the advantage of having a

lot of money deposited. 'A lot of cash. Quickly.'

'How much?' he asked.

'Half a million. Sterling.'

'Ah, that is a lot,' he said.

'I've got it.'

'And a whole lot more Mr Stark. That's not the problem.'

'Then what is?'

'The government of your country has many rules about the transfer of cash. Something to do with money laundering I believe.'

He said it as if he could hardly believe such a thing existed. But we both knew better. 'And as you know, we do not have business premises in the UK.'

'I know.' That was one of the reasons I chose that bank.

'But we do have reciprocal arrangements with one or two establishments in cases of emergency. And I imagine this is an emergency.'

'You could say that.'

'Would you like me to make enquiries then?'

'Yes,' I said, shivering in my shoes.

'Could I call you back?'

'I'd rather call you.'

'Very well. Shall we say in an hour?'

'We shall.'

'Then I'd better get busy. We'll speak then.'

'Yes,' I said, and hung up after a brief goodbye.

I nipped back to the hotel and had two bubbling hot Irish

coffees to take away the chill. But the cold lump in my stomach about what had happened to Judith just wouldn't go away. I was back at the phone box within the hour. It was empty, which didn't surprise me, the state it was in.

I got through straight away.

'Good news,' said my banker. 'But I'm afraid it's at a price.'

'Tell me,' I said.

'There's a bank in Old Street in London. You know Old Street?'

'Yes.'

He gave me an address. 'You are to see a Mr Mahood. He will have a half a million pounds for you the day after tomorrow at start of business.'

'No sooner?'

'I'm afraid not. The money has to be liquidated from various sources so as not to raise any suspicion of foul play. Ten o'clock that morning at his office. He is a reliable man. I vouch for him, even though it is not the most prepossessing building.'

'Good.'

'There is a fee of course.'

'I would never have guessed. How much?'

'Ten per cent.'

'Fifty grand?'

'That's the regular amount for a transaction such as this. Do you find it acceptable?'

'I have no choice. You'll sort that out.'

'Of course.'

I wondered how much of that would end up in his back pocket, but right then I didn't care.

'Then I'll transfer the money straight away,' he said. 'And he will do the rest.'

'Yes, thank you,' I said.

'Always a pleasure doing business with you, Mr Stark.'

'Yeah,' I said. 'And thanks again.'

'I hope the money solves any problems you may have in London.'

'So do I,' I said.

One day down, two to go.

46

Then I called the only other person in the country whose number I still had, or had mine on the island. Ex-Detective Inspector Jack Robber, now living by the seaside with his sister. Or at least he was when I left.

The phone rang for so long I thought I might have a wrong number, but eventually he picked up. 'Robber,' he said in a weak voice.

'Jack,' I said, 'It's Nick Sharman.'

'Blimey,' he said. 'Long time since I heard your voice. Where are you?'

'In London.'

'Why? I thought you were *persona non grata in* this part of the world.'

'Long story,' I said.

'I just bet it is.' I could hear the grin in his voice.

'How's your sister?' I asked.

'Dead. More than a year ago. Heart attack.'

'Christ. I'm sorry mate. You never let me know.'

'What was the point? Would you have come back for the funeral?'

'Suppose not. So how are you?'

'Not good. I'm next. Cancer of the prostate. A pain in the arse. Literally. That's why I took so long answering. I was in the khazi. Spend a lot of time there lately.'

'I don't know what to say.'

'Don't say anything. I've had a good run. People live too long these days anyway. It's like God's waiting room down here as it is.'

'How are you managing on your own?'

'Not bad. Given up on the fucking doctors. Just take the pain killers and survive on spag bol and red wine from the Spar supermarket down the road. I miss my sister, mind. The place is a bit of a tip since she went. Anyway, you didn't phone to enquire after my health. What do you want?'

'I need an oppo. Like I said a long story. Wondered if you fancied a trip up to London.'

'I don't think I'd be much good to you these days Nick. I'm not the man I was.'

'Better than nothing though. There's room here for you to stay and I think I could do better than a Spar spaghetti out of a box.'

'Where exactly are you?' he asked.

I told him.

'Nice digs,' he said.

'Expensive.'

'You always did have tastes beyond your means.'

'Fancy it then?' I asked.

'When?'

'I was thinking of tomorrow. It's kind of urgent.'

'Blimey.' He coughed. 'It must be important.'

'So?'

'Well there's a train to London at nine. I could be with you before lunch.'

'I've got no wheels to pick you up.'

'I think I can afford a cab from the station.'

'Fine. I'll be here. Name's Stark by the way. Just ask at the desk.'

'God. You never change do you?'

'I try to be consistent.'

'OK, then. I'll see you about twelve.'

'Look forward to it.'

Two days down. One to go. Jesus, it was hard this waiting. Wondering how Judith was coping.

Still, they do say that it's the time of year for families.

47

I hardly slept, worrying about Judith, just watched garbage on TV. Quiz shows, monster truck races, anything to pass the time until the next morning when I called the Russians on the mobile number I'd been given, and told them I'd have the money the day after next. 'Very good Mr Sharman,' said the thickly accented voice at the other end – which one of the bastards I didn't know, as he didn't identify himself. 'Please call as soon as you are in possession and we'll arrange a meeting. And naturally, no police.'

'And my daughter is safe.' It was a statement, not a question.

'You hardly need ask,' he replied, smugly.

'I'll need to speak to her.'

'Of course.'

'And if you...'

'No threats, Mr Sharman,' he said. 'A waste of energy I assure you.'

Don't you be so sure, I thought. Things might change when I get Judith back.

'Just don't hurt her,' I said.

'There would be no point. This is strictly business,' and he hung up.

Not wanting to be wandering the streets with that amount of cash, I phoned Stew, the cabbie. 'I need a ride the day after tomorrow in the morning,' I said.

'No probs. What time?'

'I need to get to Old Street for ten, wait and return.'

'To and from the hotel?'

'Yeah.'

'Pierre's looking after you then?'

'Very well.' I wasn't interested in going into my domestic arrangements, but then he wasn't to know.

'Good. Then I'll be with you just after nine. Traffic's awful at that time in the morning going out East.'

'I'll be waiting,' I said.

48

Trouble was, there wasn't going to be much I could do to defend myself without weapons, and mine had been confiscated by the spooks like a schoolboy having his catapults taken away. Bastards. A nailgun and a jemmy just wouldn't cut what I had in mind. So it looked like another trip to Hackney was on the cards. I'd been lucky the first time up with Skins' little firm – I hoped that they were true to his words and always *in situ*.

I waited for dark, drinking the mini bar dry and watching yet more rubbish on the box. I missed Judith, I missed the island. When the evening came I headed east in a black cab picked up off Oxford Street. He dropped me just outside Hackney Town Hall and I walked into the back streets. I had a grand in my pants again, and prayed I'd go home without it. The pub looked the same from the outside, dilapidated and miserable. It suited my mood to a T.

I pushed open the door and it looked exactly the same inside as well. The same motley crew of drinkers at the tables, and Skin, Arnold and Latimer propping up the bar. In fact there *was* one difference. The barman was now wearing a moth-eaten red and white Santa hat that looked like it had been picked out of a skip. My three buds clocked me and all started to grin. 'Hey,' said Skin. 'It's the man with the plan. Have a drink my friend.'

'Pint please,' I said as I joined them.

'So what can we do for you this evening?' he asked.

'Had a little problem,' I said. 'Lost what you got me.'

'Careless,' said Arnold, kissing his teeth.

I nodded.

'No comebacks this end though?' he questioned.

'Course not.'

'Fair enough. What do you need?'

'There's two of us,' I said. 'Or at least I hope so.' I didn't know what condition Robber was in. Prostate cancer – every man's fear. My arse cheeks clenched at the mere thought. 'But he's not the man he used to be I'm afraid. I need a shot gun. I don't need to aim, just point and pray.'

'A scatter gun,' said Skin. 'I think I can manage that. Sawn off?'

'That would be be just fine.'

'And?'

'A hand gun. Anything.'

'Nine mill?'

'Sure.'

'Expensive. Short notice too.'

'Just tell me.'

Skin thought for a moment, doing some mental calculations. 'Seven fifty with ammo.'

Vicious, but fair. 'Bring it on,' I said.

'Be back soon,' he said, and he and Latimer left me with Arnold. We swapped reminiscences about the island again, and truth to tell it made me feel homesick for another place in my own home town.

The pair returned after an hour or so. 'Outside,' said Skin.

I followed him into the night and to his car, a late model seven-series BMW. 'Business is good,' I said, clocking his motor.

'Could be worse.'

We sat inside and he opened a sports bag which contained a beaten up sawn off shotgun with a taped handle and a decent looking Browning automatic. 'They work fine,' he said, seeing my expression as I looked at the ragged shotgun. 'Trust me.' I had no choice.

There was ammunition for both and I hauled the cash out of my jeans an counted out seven hundred and fifty quid. 'Still warm,' said Skin.

'Close to my heart.'

'You'd better split,' he said. 'Don't want the stuff hanging about too long. Babylon's getting busy. Too many folks shot in this yard lately. You driving?'

I shook my head.

'There's a mini cab firm on the corner.'

'Sure,' I replied. 'Give my best to the boys.'

'Will do. Will we see you again do you think?'

'I hope not. I want to be spending the holidays back on the island. It's too cold here for me.'

'Well, good luck, whatever happens.'

'Same to you, and Merry Christmas.'

'Back at you,' He gave me a complicated handshake, and with that I got out of the car and headed for the cab office.

49

The next morning I was up bright and early, hoping that Robber was as good as his word. I couldn't settle in the suite, so I sat in reception waiting for him and ambushed him before he got to the desk. 'Jack,' I said, holding out my hand. 'It's good to see you.'

He took the proffered mitten and we shook hands. 'Good to see you too Mr *Stark*. But I don't know if I'd have recognised you with that growth on your face.'

I'd've recognised *him* anywhere. He was older, greyer, thinner, but still the old enemy who'd become one of my only friends. We'd got up to some larkins in the old days. I'd been his snout for a while, earning a bit on the side when the PI business was on its uppers, and the booze bill was due. He was the epitome of the straight copper who looked the other way when it suited him. Good old Jack.

He was wearing an ancient trilby and a mac that had seen better days, and carrying a small leather bag. 'I brought my jammies,' he said. 'It's been a long time since I've stayed in a place like this.'

'You're welcome mate,' I said. 'I thought we'd go upstairs. It's more private, and we can eat on room service.'

'Very grand. Lead the way.'

We went up in the lift to the suite, which he gave a nod of approval, and I took his hat and coat and put them in Judith's room with his bag. 'Drink?' I said when I came back into the sitting room.

'Scotch. Large one. Can't afford the hard stuff on my pension. Shouldn't though, the quacks tell me.'

'You sure about that Scotch then?'

'Fuck the fucking doctors. I'm too far gone for it to do too much harm.'

'Fair enough.' I poured him a large one, and one for myself from the mini bar. When I handed him his glass I noticed his hand was shaking. Not a good sign in a number two shooter, but he was all I had.

'So, what's the problem?' he asked.

'It's about Judith,' I replied.

'Guessed as much.' Robber nodded thoughtfully. 'I've followed her career, and her recent problems.'

I raised an eyebrow. More difficult than you might think as it happens.

'I still have contacts,' he said. 'Keep my ear to the grapevine if you know what I mean.'

I nodded.

'As it happens, I was going to get in touch with her.' Robber continued. 'But then I thought she would hardly remember me, and what would she want from an old bloke like me anyway.'

'Some support,' I huffed, though I could hardly have expected him to do any more.

'I can hardly support myself these days mate. Times are hard. Anyway, my troubles are not what you brought me to hear. What can I do for you?'

'Point a gun in someone's face,' I said. Then I told him what had happened.

He listened patiently as I went through the story, from finding the memory stick, meeting Campbell's lover to Judith being kidnapped. All he said when I'd finished was, 'I always thought that new AC was a piece of stupid shit.'

'He's not the problem now,' I said. 'It's the Russians.'

'And you can't find the people you gave the photographs to?'

'Gone without a trace,' I said. 'No point in even looking. And no time.'

'No idea which department?'

'Not a clue. They weren't forthcoming.'

'Fucking spooks never are, but they always expect full co-operation from the force when they need it.'

'Way of the world,' I said.

'Shitty world,' he said.

I nodded again. Just having Robber around made me feel a little calmer, but I would only be satisfied when I knew that Judith was safe.

50

By the time I'd finished filling him in it was getting on one o'clock. I poured two more drinks and asked if he wanted to eat.

'Is the Pope a bear?' he said.

'What do you fancy?'

'Steak and chips,' he said, with no hesitation. 'Medium rare, with jam roly poly and custard for afters.'

I picked up the phone and ordered a T-Bone and French fries, with all the trimmings. Jam roly poly wasn't on the menu, but they offered some kind of sponge pudding with a raspberry cômpote and vanilla sauce, so I took that instead. I wasn't hungry. My stomach was in knots, so I just asked for some soup and a roll. However little I felt like eating, I knew I had to have something just to keep my strength up and the liquor down. Soup seemed the easiest thing to digest. I also asked for a large pot of coffee and hot milk.

While we waited Robber asked, 'Have you got the money?'

'I'm due to pick it up tomorrow morning.'

'Not easy to get that much at short notice.'

'I have my sources.' I thought it was better for him not to know too much about this side of the deal.

'When's the exchange?'

'Soon as I have the cash.'

'You think they've hurt her?'

'No. We've spoken. She's as mad as a cat who's swallowed a wasp, but she seems OK.'

'The old Sharman spirit eh?' he said.

'That's about it.'

'But you don't trust them?'

'Would you trust them?'

'And I'm all you've got?'

'That pretty much covers it.'

'I don't know Nick.'

'Listen Jack. I didn't know about your condition when I called. Why didn't you ever get in touch? You had the number.'

'And spoil your life in paradise? No fear. Anyway you couldn't have done anything about it.'

'Yeah, I know. I've missed out on a lot being out there. Look, just forget about it. Stay here tonight, keep me company. Believe me, I could use someone here or else I'll be biting the furniture. Then go home tomorrow and I'll go on my own. No hard feelings.'

'What, and miss all the fun?' he said, and laughed so loudly his false teeth clicked. 'I'm an old man with a crap pension and dodgy prostate. Bring on a bit of excitement, I say.'

We were interrupted by a knock on the door. When I answered it, two white coated waiters brought in a trolley covered in dishes under silver lids. They laid the table for two, put out the food with a flourish and stood back proudly. Robber watched with wide eyes as they revealed a sizzling steak that had been kept hot by a paraffin stove. It was so big it overlapped the plate. The chips were jumbo size and brown as my face. There was a side order of mixed vegetables and a salad. The pudding was also kept warm next to a big jug of sauce. My soup and roll looked pathetic next to his feast and my stomach rumbled.

'Marvellous,' he said, taking his seat as one of the waiters dropped a napkin on his lap. 'I could get used to this.'

I tipped the chaps a fiver each and joined Robber at the table.

'The condemned men ate a hearty meal,' he said, as he sliced a lump off the steak.

'Nice choice of words,' I replied, hoping that they wouldn't turn out to be true.

51

'So what's the plan?' said Robber.

'Simple,' I said. 'We drive to the meet. You wait outside with the money and the shotgun. I get Judith. They get the money. We go home.'

'Sounds easy,' he said, frowning.

'It will be – unless they piss me off, or they do a double cross. Then we kill them. Or maybe we kill them anyway.'

'I thought you didn't have wheels.'

'I don't. But I will. You can get anything in this hotel.' I picked up the phone and called the desk. Pierre answered. 'Hey Pierre,' I said. 'I need to hire a car.'

'No problem Mr Stark. What particular car?'

'Something with a big boot.'

'A Bentley Continental?'

'I think a Bentley's a bit ostentatious,' I said. 'But a nice idea.'

'Perhaps a Jaguar sedan.'

'That will do I'm sure. There's two drivers.' I looked over at Robber. 'I hope you still have a driving license,' I said to him.

'Never go anywhere without it.'

'Yes, two drivers,' I said into the dog.

'When do you require the car?' Pierre asked.

'Quick as you can.'

'I'll have someone come up with the paperwork,' he said.

We both hung up and I said, 'See what I mean?'

'Why do you need a big boot?' asked Robber.

'Because that's where you'll be.'

'Are you serious?' he spluttered.

'It won't be for long. And it's a Jag.'

'I think I'd have preferred the Bentley,' he said.

52

Half an hour later, one of the reception staff appeared with some forms to fill in to hire the Jaguar.

I used my fake driving licence in the name of Stark, Jack used his legal one. The receptionist took us down to the garage where the car was parked. 'Are you familiar with the model?' he asked.

Neither of us were, so he ran through the controls until he was satisfied we knew where the indicators and windscreen wipers were, then handed over the keys. 'Thanks a lot,' I said, tipping him the usual blue bank note.

Jack and I went back upstairs where he told me he was taking a nap. 'Right old git aren't I?' he said. 'Not like the old days when I could stay up night after night on the piss.'

'We all get older Jack,' I said.

'Not much older for me,' he said as he headed for his

room. It hurt me to hear him talk like that, just as much as the change in his appearance. The fact of the matter is that some of us don't get older. I'd seen enough people die to know that. And almost died myself as a matter of fact. Suddenly the room was colder.

I considered driving the car myself to Old Street to pick up the cash, but what I'd seen of morning traffic around the town told me to stick to the cab I'd booked. Besides I didn't want to be bothered with parking, and the possibility of having the motor towed away. I didn't fancy having to report it at the local cop shop. Jack reappeared around six, looking all the better for his siesta.

'I'm going to get the cash first thing,' I said.

'Want me to come?'

No. I've got a cab coming. You sleep in mate, save your strength. Have a decent breakfast. We don't know what fun and games these people have got in store for us.

'Fine by me,' he said, helping himself to a scotch. 'Now, what do you fancy for supper?'

For a dying man he had a hell of an appetite, but I thought it better not to say so. This was the calm before the storm, I could feel it in my bones. These fucking Russians were taking the piss. Kidnapping my daughter was against all the rules. Fuck their photos and videos, fuck the money. And fuck them.

I knew it was all going to go pear shaped, and I could see that Jack knew it too. He was like some old gunfighter in a film, going on his last hurrah.

I just hoped I was wrong.

53

I was up and waiting in reception for Stew the cabbie to pick me up by quarter to nine. I'd had no sleep and was red eyed, my tan turned a sickly yellow. I couldn't face breakfast, just enough coffee to get my synapse wired. Couldn't even bother with the paper, or the crossword, so I knew things were bad.

He came through the doors just after nine. By then the inside of my mouth was sore from chewing at the skin.

He saw me across the room and came over. Took one look and said 'Heavy night?'

'You could say that,' I replied.

'Traffic's not too bad,' he said. 'But better get moving. Old Street, you said?'

I gave him the number.

'We'll find it.'

As it happened the traffic was quite light and we made good time. We were in Old Street by five to ten, and he scanned the shops and offices for the right number. 'There you go,' Stew said, pointing to a shabby greengrocer's shop. 'Getting some fruit?' He looked at me quizzically.

'No,' I said through the plastic divider. 'It'll be upstairs.'

'Right,' he said. 'I'll be here, or close by if a fucking warden gets on my case.'

'Just don't leave,' I said sternly. The last thing I needed was to be stranded with £500K in used bills.

'Wouldn't dream of it.'

I got out of the cab and went over to the building. There was a scuffed black door next to the shop with the number on it in peeling paint. No sign of any kind of business inside. On one side of the door was an entry buzzer, which I pressed. A voice answered with a single 'Yes.'

'Jim Stark for Mr Mahood,' I said, and the buzzer sounded. I pushed open the door to reveal a dusty, bare staircase heading upwards, illuminated by a single bulb. I climbed the stairs until I came to a half glass door. There was still no sign of life and the staircase went further up. But there were no more lights, so I pushed open the door. Inside was a bare white room, its window covered by a white shade. The carpet was dark grey. In the middle of the room was a brown wooden desk. The top was bare too. Nothing. No phone, computer or papers. Behind the desk was a black leather swivel chair. The only other things in the office were two cheap looking *faux* leather suitcases. When I entered the man in the chair stood. He was tall, young, dark skinned, immaculately dressed in a three-piece suit, white shirt and red tie. 'Mr Stark,' he said, obviously expecting me.

'Mr Mahood,' I replied.

He nodded, and we shook hands. His was firm and dry, mine was firm and damp, but he at least had the good manners not to wipe his hands on his trousers. Or maybe he thought my sweat was acidic and would ruin the material.

'I have your money,' he said, and nodded in the direction of the cases. 'Fifties and twenties. Bundled in lots of five K. You may count it if you wish.'

I shook my head. 'My banker vouched for you,' I said.

'As I would for him in similar circumstances.'

'Do you want ID?' I asked.

'He described you to me. No ID necessary,' Mahood said coolly, in his East London accent. He went to the bags, opened the zips and opened the lids.

Lots of cash, banded. I picked up a few bundles and flipped through them. All money. No newspaper cut up into note-sized lumps. Kosher. But then I knew my banker, and he knew me. We had an understanding. He knew that if he fucked with me, there would be trouble. Big trouble. You don't hide that sort of money in his sort of bank without there being something of a nasty back story. 'So that's it,' I said. 'Nothing to sign?'

He smiled. 'No paperwork. I have been paid my commission. The transaction is complete.'

I didn't ask how much his commission had actually been – it would have been rude.

'That's it then.' I fastened the cases tight, and humped them once. It's surprising how heavy money can be. 'Feels right,' I said.

'I hope it solves any problem you may have.'

'So do I,' I said. We shook hands again and I left.

Stew was parked in the same place. I hefted the bags into the back of the cab and we headed back to the hotel. Job done.

54

When I got back to the hotel with the cases, Jack was up and enjoying a lavish breakfast, just like I'd said. 'Coffee?' he asked.

'Sure.' The sight of the food had finally made me hungry. 'But I've got to make a call first.'

'That the money?' he said.

'That's it Jack. Want to see?'

'Half a million in cold cash.' His eyes lit up. 'Too right. Not often I'll get a chance to see that much cash.'

I opened both bags and he weighed some of the packets in his hands. 'You had a result that time didn't you?' He was referring to my bank robbing days.

'For what it's worth,' I said. 'I'd rather have a family.'

'You will. Now make that call and let's get this baby put to bed.'

I did as he said and called up the number I'd been given by the Russians.

When a man answered I said, without preamble, 'She'd better be all right.'

'In the pink,' said the garbled accent. These bastards certainly knew some old English expressions. Probably watching too much *EastEnders*.

'Let me speak to her.'

'You have the money.'

'I do. Let me speak to my daughter,' I repeated.

The phone went dead, Judith came on. 'Dad,' she said. 'You OK?'

'if you think staying with these soap dodging bastards is OK. Talk about strangers to deodorant.' She was OK.

'They've not hurt you?' I asked tentatively.

'No. Their mum's kept them on a short leash.'

'Mum?'

'Oh yeah, like that sodding spook said, it's a family affair. Hold on, Georgie wants a word.'

Georgie, I thought. She was getting matey and I smiled at the thought of my cunning daughter, able to disarm anyone.

The Russian came back on. 'Satisfied?' he said.

'I will be when I get my daughter back.'

'Then bring the money here, now.' He gave me an address in Knightsbridge, just round the corner. 'And no police – or you know what will happen.'

'You got it,' I said, and he hung up.

55

It was time to rock and roll. Jack and I carried the cases of money and the sports bag with the two loaded guns down to the garage. 'You really want me in the boot?' said Jack. 'A man in my condition?'

'Can't think of any other way,' I retorted. 'There's still time for you to back out. Like I said, no hard feelings.'

'Well try and make it quick,' he said huffing. 'Bleedin hell.'

We put the bags in the boot and I drove to Knightsbridge, with Jack in the passenger seat next to me. I found the street, part of a leafy square with parking meters next to a high iron fence and pulled in. I filled the meter with change which made it legal for two hours. The last thing I wanted was for the motor to be towed away with Jack inside, complete with illegal weapons and half a million quid in cash. I didn't mention the thought.

The boot was spacious enough to fit his body inside plus the pistol and shotgun next to the cases. 'I really am sorry about this Jack,' I said, looking up and down the street. 'Do it,' I said, when the coast was clear.

'Bollocks,' he said as he slipped into the space. 'Now fuck off and get sorted.'

I crossed the road and rang the bell for the apartment number I'd been given over the phone. A guttural voice answered. 'It's me,' I said, and I was buzzed in.

The flat was on the top floor and I took the lift to a private foyer.

I was met by a squat, well built geezer in a bad suit with a pistol in his german, who frisked me down in a professional way. 'I come in peace,' I said, but thought *if you believe that, you'll believe anything.*

When he was satisfied I was unarmed, he stepped away from me which was a relief as, just like Judith had said, he seemed to be a stranger to soap and water. 'Where is the money?' he demanded.

'Close,' I said. 'But first I want to see my daughter.'

He gave me a filthy look, but backed through another door into the apartment proper. I followed him.

The penthouse flat was a thing of beauty – if your tastes ran to gold leaf dining table and chairs, etched glass doors to the balcony, and a carpet so deep that it gave my shoes a polish as I walked on it. But on a closer look, the place was uncared for. There was dust on the surfaces, the windows were dirty and smeared, the carpet was stained and the whole place stank of chips and body odour. Not that I'm the perfect housewife, but one does have standards. And these bad boys obviously did not.

There was a chair with its back against the balcony window so that it was in silhouette, with someone sitting in it. 'Mama,' said the bloke who'd let me in. And then something in Russian. About the lack of cash, I imagined.

'There's money,' I said. 'As long as my daughter's safe.'

'She's safe,' said the woman as she rose from her chair and walked towards me so that I could see her properly. I wished she hadn't.

She was three stone overweight, stuffed into a dress three sizes too small. The tops of her breasts were on show, but they were wrinkled and flabby, and I could just imagine the cellulite creeping up her fat thighs. On her head was perched possibly the worst Irish I'd ever seen. It was platinum blonde in colour and looked like it was made from steel wool. Not a good look, particularly as I could swear there were bugs crawling about inside it. Something was moving inside it, that was for sure, and I thought it better not to look too closely. And if she wanted to perpetuate the belief that she was a natural blonde she should have done something about the grey hairs sprouting from the massive wart on her chin. Her lips were thin and mean and when she opened her mouth I was certain that her teeth were made from wood, so darkly stained were they. A real doll.

'Mr Sharman,' she said with a smile as false as her Hampsteads. 'At last we meet.'

'A pleasure,' I said.

'I wish I could believe you. Now, you're sure you have our money.'

'I have it,' I said. 'It's safe until I'm sure my daughter is the same.'

'We have no intention of cheating you,' she said. 'And your daughter is just fine.'

'Let me see her.'

'Let me see the money.'

'My daughter first.'

She smiled and showed more discoloured teeth. 'An *impasse*,' she said, cruelly. 'But we have the upper hand I think. Georgie,' she said to her son as she showed me the little belly gun she was holding. 'Fetch Alexie and the girl.' Then to me. 'You see Mr Sharman, we are not intractable. We both have children we love. We are not barbarians.'

Like fuck, I thought. Just get me my daughter, unharmed, you ugly cunt.

56

Georgie left the room through another door, as Mum kept me covered with her pistol. 'What were you thinking Mr Sharman?' she said. 'Surely you must have known that stealing those photographs would only bring you trouble.'

'I try not to think too far into the future,' I replied. 'Gives me a headache.'

'Not the wisest of philosophies.'

'Served me OK so far.' I said, shortly. 'How did you find us by the way?'

'We have friends in high places.'

'Spooks,' I said.

'Perhaps. Perhaps not.'

It was the fucking spooks all right. Bastards would sell their own mothers for peanuts. I had a feeling Judith and I had been set up. And by Christ someone was going to pay.

The door opened again and Georgie, accompanied by another ugly little bastard, came in, Judith between them. She looked OK, but I could tell she wasn't happy.

'You see,' said Mum. 'No damage.'

'Bitch bit me,' said the other man, who I assumed was brother Alexie.

'Nearly died of food poisoning too,' said Judith. 'Hello Dad. Welcome to Minsk.'

'Shut up,' said Georgie. 'You always making bloody jokes. What's so bloody funny?'

'Your dress sense for one thing,' replied Judith.

'Bitch,' said Georgie. 'Fucking funny bitch. Never quiet. Needs sorting by a real man.'

'Pity there's none in your family,' said Judith.

I thought he was going to whack her then. 'Caught it off me,' I said. 'I never know when to shut up either.'

'Then get us the money,' said Alexie. 'And get the fuck out of our faces.'

'A pleasure,' I said. 'It's downstairs in my car.'

'Then let's get it,' said Georgie. 'And this business can be all over.'

'Suits me,' I said. 'Come on then.'

We left, Georgie carrying his pistol stuck in his suit coat pocket. It didn't improve the hang of the jacket, but did make it hard for him to shoot anyone right off. I could only pray as he went downstairs that Jack hadn't lost his bottle – and that the street was quiet enough to carry out the plan without being disturbed.

57

'A lot of pounds to leave lying around in the street?' said Georgie when we got outside.

'It's only money,' I replied.

'I like that attitude,' he said, baring his dirty teeth in a smile. 'You won't miss it then.'

I just shrugged. He was enjoying his day, but I was just about to piss on his parade big time.

He made me walk in front of him, the pistol still in his jacket pocket. I took the key fob for the Jag from my pocket and pointed it at the back of the car. 'In the boot,' I directed him.

'No problem.' He moved up to my side, and I could see he was almost salivating at the thought of the cash. I looked round and the street was deserted, so I popped the boot lid. As he stuck his beak inside, Robber popped up like a literal Jack-in-the-box with the sawn-off in his hands. 'You, fucker,' he said to Georgie, whose mouth hung open, 'let's see your hands. And as for you Sharman, you took your fucking time didn't you. I can hardly feel my legs in here.' All of a sudden he sounded like the old Jack Robber that I used to know.

'Sorry, mate,' I said. 'Couldn't drag myself away from the company. Now Georgie, hand out of pocket. Empty. There's a good boy.'

He growled but did as he was told, and I helped myself to his gun. A nice Glock 9mm, which was certainly cleaner than his flat.

I kept looking round for anyone paying us attention, the last thing I needed was any nosy cops appearing. 'Come on Jack,' I said. 'Out you get. And keep that shooter out of sight for Christ's sake.'

'Gimme a chance,' he said, clambering out awkwardly. 'You know the state of me.'

'You're a fucking star Jack,' I said, poking Georgie hard in the back with his own gun. 'Come on son, let's go and see your mummy.'

58

'So how's Judith?' asked Jack when he was back on *terra firma*.

'Not happy, but not too bad. She bit Georgie here's brother.'

'Good for her. Right Mr Sharman, what now?'

'Now, we go and get her.'

'And the money?'

'Hand it over. I want this thing done and dealt with, and no comebacks.'

'So why all this?' He looked perplexed, indicated to the guns in our hands.

'Just so they know we're not worth messing with again. Georgie,' I said. 'You carry the cash.'

He hauled the two suitcases out of the boot and I slammed it shut. 'Come on then,' I said. 'Off we go.'

We went back to the block of flats and used Georgie's security key to get the lift to the penthouse. He carried the suitcases into the flat where Alexie, Mum and Judith were waiting. Jack showed the room the shotgun and I held up Georgie's gun in my hand. 'Weapons on the floor,' I ordered, 'and no messing about.'

'You stupid boy,' said Mum to Georgie. 'How could you let this happen?'

He didn't reply, but looked at the floor.

'Weapons,' I said again, tapping my foot impatiently.

Alexie pulled out another Glock and it hit the carpet, next to mum's little pistol. 'That's good,' I said, picking them up, Robber's shotgun covering me, directed straight at them. 'Now let's all just relax, and we'll be leaving.'

'Is that Mr Robber?' asked Judith, looking pleased. She'd always seen Jack as a grandfather figure.

'In the flesh,' he replied. 'How are you love?'

'All the better for seeing you,' she said, before planting her fist square into Georgie's face. 'I've been wanting to do that for days,' she said, sounding satisfied.

That's when it all kicked off.

59

Something snapped in Georgie when Judith punched him, and he went right for her throat with both of his meaty hands. He smashed her against the wall, so I fired the Glock. The bullet slammed into the plaster next to them, but he didn't let go. I couldn't risk firing again for risk of hitting her so I ran across the floor and slugged him hard on the back of the neck with the pistol's barrel. Only then did he release the pressure on Judith, but in all the commotion, Alexie pulled a small revolver from an ankle holster and levelled it at me. But before he'd had the chance to fire Jack pulled the trigger on the scatter gun, blowing most of Alexie's head off his shoulders. That really got to Mum, who threw herself across the carpet screaming blue bloody murder, hell bent on reaching the gun that had fallen from his hand. It was my turn then, and I fired the Glock again. The first bullet hit her between the shoulder blades, the second knocked the wig from her head, exposing balding grey hair. She never even got to the gun. Just lay with her twitching outstretched fingers inches from the butt.

Georgie *really* lost it then and came at me hard. I hit the carpet and knew he had to die too or we'd never see the end of this, so I put one shot into his open mouth and the back of his skull. Most of his brain joined his brother's across the balcony window. He fell beside me and I rolled over and on to my feet.

'Now why the fuck did you hit him?' I said to Judith through the haze of smoke, cordite stench and coppery smell of blood.

'It seemed like a good idea at the time,' she replied, although I could hardly hear for the ringing in my ears from the gunfire.

'Well, whatever. But I think it's time for us to go, don't you?' I looked at the three bodies on the thick carpet which was fast soaking up the spilt blood. They hadn't even managed to get one shot off between them. The three of us were stinking of cordite, and there were gory splatters on our clothes.

We gathered all the weapons – both theirs and ours – and carried them out in a couple of black sacks I found in the kitchen, and Judith collected her coat and from the room where they'd kept her prisoner. She pulled her coat over the blood on her dress, and Jack and I cleaned ourselves up as best we could in the bathroom. Before we left I gave her back her mobile.

She switched it on, and checked something. 'Well, just fancy that,' she said.

'What?' I asked.

'Later. This place is giving me the creeps, let's get out of here.'

The last thing I did before we left the room was put Mum's wig straight. 'Don't want you having a bad hair day do we?' I said, as we left the building, carrying the suitcases back to the motor.

60

The whole block was silent as we headed back to the car. It might just as well have been completely empty – perhaps it was. Same deal in the street. Just a couple of pedestrians and some passing cars, but no sign of any cops. Seemed like no one had noticed the commotion in the penthouse we'd just left – guess people round here tended to keep to themselves. Thank Christ for triple glazing, I thought. We stuffed the swag in the boot of the Jag, and drove back to Park Lane, Jack Robber proudly at the wheel. 'So, what now?' he asked.

'Me, I'm off home,' I said. 'Back to the island. If I can get a flight tonight I can be in the States tomorrow, call up my pilot friend and be back in time for a late Christmas lunch.'

'Can't you stay another day?' asked Judith.

'No darling,' I said. 'I told you. I don't belong here any more.'

'You might get a pull at the airport,' she warned. 'Don't forget what that spook said about facial recognition software.'

'It's the day before Christmas,' I said. 'The place will be heaving. And I'm going, not coming. Anyway, if I *do* get nicked, well that's life. I'll take my chances.'

'And the money?'

'I'm not humping that about. Hey Jack. Take one of the bags as a thank you. And Judith, you have the other. Merry Christmas.'

'A quarter of a million,' said Jack, his eyes wide. 'Christ, Nick, are you sure?'

'Like I said to that Russian, Jack, it's only money. I've got plenty more.'

'What can I say?'

'Say nothing mate. I couldn't have done it without you. Call it your payment, You'd better take the motor too. You can take it back to any Hertz office. Or keep the bloody thing. Have some fun. Enjoy yourself.'

'I'll do that all right. Might even get my leg over. It's been a long time.'

'Too much information, Jack,' said Judith, laughing.

'And get rid of those bloody guns will you?' I said.

'No problem.'

We went to the hotel, sliding through the back entrance so as not to attract any attention and Jack collected his things. Judith dived into a shower and got changed before we all had a last drink together.

As he was leaving he said, wistfully, 'I doubt we'll meet again.'

'Probably not,' I said. 'But who knows? You might fancy a trip to the Caribbean. You've got the cash for a ticket now, anyway.'

'No.' he replied. 'Better like this. Both of us still standing. Judith. You take care. Keep in touch love.'

'I will,' she said, and Jack shook my hand, gave Judith a hug and left, after one final Merry Christmas to us both.

'So,' I said to my daughter. 'This is it.'

'Looks like it Dad.'

'I won't say it's been fun, but I'm glad I came.'

'Me too, believe me.'

'So it's Christmas as usual.'

'Yeah. I need to get some stuff. Presents. You know. Sorry I haven't got anything for you.'

'You're all I need.'

'Still the charmer eh Dad?'

'It's the truth.'

'I know.'

'So tell me, who did kill that snout of yours. Are you any the wiser?' I asked.

'Those two bloody Russian idiots,' she replied, shaking her head. 'They didn't realise what a pair of total arseholes they were. Went round to Tommy's flat after he'd copied those photos and fucked their hard drive. He thought they didn't know where he lived. Only sensible thing they did was keeping tabs on the poor sod, it seems. They were so wired on booze and coke that Alexie pulled the trigger before they had a chance to find out where he'd hidden the memory stick.'

'So how did they find us?'

'That Scottish spook bastard gave them a heads up.'

'Charming. So what about you?' I asked.

'I'm golden. Got a text – I've been fully exonerated of all charges. Back on duty the day after Boxing Day. But it's traffic. Uniform. Their way of telling me I'm not totally off the hook.'

'You going to do it?' I asked.

'Dunno. Like I said, I was thinking about putting in my papers. And now with all that cash...'

'Well remember what I told you. I mean it, you're always welcome at mine. Who knows, you might even meet a nice bloke on the island.'

'We'll see Dad. Anyway, got to go. Get the car and head off to Kent.'

'Merry Christmas then,' I said. 'I love you.'

'Love you too. Always will,' she said.

We hugged tightly and Judith left in her car with the case of money.

So that was that.

61

So all I had left to do was to pay my bill and find my way home. Home. Now there's a word. For so long, London had always been the place I thought of as home. Even when I was on the island, baking myself in the sun and listening to Reggae, Ska, Bluebeat, jazz and old rock and roll records at Clive's bar on that old jukebox. But after this trip, I knew it wasn't – not any more. The island was my home, and I hoped it always would be. Maybe I'd even get a visitor after all this time. And maybe Judith would go back to being a copper, and just make the occasional phone call to me.

I called up Stew the cabbie. 'You working?' I asked.

'Always. Gotta keep the wolf from the door.'

'Fancy a run to the airport?'

'Course. What time's your flight?'

'Small problem. Don't have one yet. Just fancied going home for the holidays. See a few folks. Missing the place.'

'Your job's finished then I take it? You'll be lucky getting a flight on Christmas Eve, mind you.'

'Oh there'll be something. Just need to get back. If necessary I'll hire a private jet.'

'Blimey. I'll expect a decent tip then.'

'You got it mate. Now listen, I'm going to have a good lunch and a bit of a drink. Got some things to celebrate. Then I'll settle up here. Give us a shout about four, yeah?'

'Consider it done,' he said, as we both hung up.

So I did just that. Pierre got more cash, and seemed very happy with my residency. No blood on the walls anyway.

I left most of the clothes I'd bought in the wardrobe – I'm sure someone would have found a use for them – but kept the overcoat as it was freezing outside. I pulled on my old jeans and boots, threw a few bits into my bag and left.

Couldn't wait to get away if truth be known.

At four I got a call that my cab was waiting outside.

62

Nick Sharman left the hotel with his one bag in his hand, into the light snow that was just beginning to fall. The streets were wet and slippery, but still crowded with shoppers heading home and punters looking for a few Christmas Eve drinks. The doorman pointed at Stew's cab. 'Your driver's waiting. Going to the airport?'

'That's right.'

'Bad night for travelling.'

Sharman pulled up his coat collar. 'Could be better,' he said. 'But I'll be in the sunshine soon enough.'

'Lucky you. Christmas dinner on the beach?'

'You got it.'

'Did you enjoy your stay?'

'It had its moments.'

'Well have a good flight. And a Merry Christmas to you.'

'Same to you.' And Nick handed him a ten pound note.

'Thank you sir. Now you be careful.'

'Always am.'

But he was wrong. As he headed across the wide pavement towards the waiting taxi, a ragged-looking man approached him. 'Got any spare change sir?' he asked in a foreign accent.

'As it happens, yes,' said Sharman, reaching into the pocket of his coat for the few coins there. With one hand holding his bag, and the other trapped by material, the man spoke again, his voice harsher now. 'You shot the wrong Russians,' he growled, producing a silenced .22 calibre automatic from under his jacket and shot Sharman twice in the chest. He opened his mouth to speak, but instead lost his balance and fell to the pavement. The ragged man put another bullet into his head, then, under the astonished looks from passing pedestrians, the doorman of the hotel, and Stew the cabbie, vanished into the crowds.

63

At around the same time on Christmas Eve, DI Judith Sharman was driving down the A2 on her way to Kent to see her friends for Christmas, hastily purchased and wrapped presents on the back seat of her car, when a Range Rover fitted with steel bumpers clipped the back of the vehicle. 'Oh shit,' she said, as she hit her emergency blinkers and pulled onto the hard shoulder followed by the truck.

She exited her car and walked back as the front passenger door of the Range Rover opened. A masked figure emerged, holding a suppressed automatic pistol. Judith turned to run back to her car but was swiftly cut down by two bullets in her back. The shooter walked over and put another bullet into the back of her head before returning to his vehicle which drove off and got lost in the traffic.

It was later discovered that her flat had been broken into that same afternoon.

★ ★ ★

The hired Jaguar was discovered burnt out in The Bluebell Woods near Guildford the day after Boxing Day. Jack Robber was identified by dental records as the deceased driver, who had been shot at point blank range twice in the head.

No money or weapons were ever recovered.

No one was ever arrested for any of the three killings.

END